NECESSARY SACRIFICE

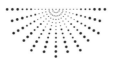

NOELLE WINTERS

Necessary Sacrifice
By Noelle Winters
Many thanks to everyone who has supported me throughout this.
All rights reserved.
Sign up for my mailing list to hear about new releases and special
offers!
http://eepurl.com/cwCSub

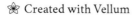 Created with Vellum

CONTENTS

REMEMBER ME

CHAPTER ONE

Tuesday, September 13th, 2016. 12:52am.

It was the burning in her arm that woke her. It felt like a fire just under her skin. She tossed her head to the side, suddenly aware of the dull pulse of pain in her head. Had she been hit? What had happened?

Then she heard a noise. She didn't lift her head, she just opened her eyes. But it was dark. She was blindfolded.

The noise continued. She could hear him.

Pacing.

She could picture him, what he was doing, having seen him do it so many times. He would pick a circle, a path, and walk it, chewing his nails, his hair greasy and his eyes wide. His appearance would be the opposite of his normal, professional self. But there was nothing that helped when he was like this. He was too far gone.

How had she fallen in love with him? That felt like so long ago. Maybe he would let her go. But she doubted it.

The fire in her arm started radiating up to her shoulder and down to her palm. She bit back a whimper, not wanting to alert him that she was awake. What had he done to her arm? How had he found her? No one was supposed to know where she was staying.

Then again, he was a powerful man. He could get access to records that others couldn't.

She closed her eyes behind the blindfold, trying not to let tears escape. She wasn't going to make it out of there, was she?

Him pinning her to the wall, his forearm to her throat.

Throwing a beer bottle at her, swearing.

Begging her to stay. Swearing he loved her. Buying her her favorite trinket.

Throwing her across the room - in the apartment he paid for - because she showed up two minutes late.

Love was blind, and she was proof. How had she loved someone who treated her like that?

"Why did you run?" His voice was scattered, distracted. Did he realize she was awake or was he talking to himself?

She heard him move closer, felt his thin fingers tugging at the knot at the back of her head. She held her breath. She hadn't seen him in six months. She had never wanted to see him again. So when the blindfold fell off, she didn't open her eyes.

"Why did you run?" he repeated.

He was talking to her. She wasn't sure what to say.

You hurt me.

I hated you.

I loved you.

None of the options would help.

She swallowed thickly, her thoughts flashing back to her friends. Her work. Would they miss her? What would her funeral be like?

"Why aren't you answering me?" He wasn't shouting. Were they close to other people, where someone might hear? Not that it mattered. She was dead anyway.

"I have nothing to say," she said softly. Her arm was pulsing with heat, her head thudding. She was getting tired now. Maybe she had always been tired.

He didn't like her answer. His footsteps were angry, walking that same path.

She gathered what adrenaline she could. Maybe she could escape. Maybe she could run. Her heart was beating fast. She held her breath, ignoring the pulsing in her head and the burning in her arm.

She pushed herself off the couch and stumbled to her feet, heading towards what she hoped was the door. Her eyes adjusted faster than she expected, but the only source of light was a small fire in the fireplace.

She couldn't even see any moonlight. Where was she? Her condo didn't have a fireplace.

An arm wrapped around her waist, pulling her roughly backwards until she could feel his body behind her. "Scream, and I'll kill you."

I'm already dead.

She closed her eyes. This was the end, and she knew it. She went limp.

One last shot.

His arms slackened. Did he think she had fainted? She hoped so. She tried not to breathe.

Then she twisted away from him and ran for it. The world crashed down on her. The door was the last thing she saw.

CHAPTER TWO

Tuesday, September 13th, 2016. 5:43pm.

Nick sat at her desk in the police station, her feet propped up on the ridiculous orthopedic thing Spencer had gotten her for Christmas. At least Spencer had gotten it in neutral colors instead of the bright blue one his eight-year-old daughter had suggested. Her computer was in front of her, with like sixteen tabs open. The computer equivalent of paperwork. Everyone thought a detective's work was glorious. Chasing down killers, kicking down doors. No one thought about the paperwork.

She looked at the desk opposite hers. Spencer sat there, all forty-something with salt-and-pepper hair. Dignified and stuff. He looked like a Detective, with a capital D. Nick looked like a college student, despite the fact that she was going on thirty. It wasn't necessarily a good thing in her job.

Spencer was talking to a lawyer, one of the district attorney's folks. The assistant district attorneys, or ADAs, were in charge of prosecuting a lot of the cases that fell into the county's jurisdiction. Consequently, they frequently came by the station to talk to the detectives.

Nick looked down at her computer, ignoring Spencer and whoever he was talking to. Eric, or something like that. Most of the ADAs had generic male names.

"Paperwork." Nick huffed, redirecting her attention. It was the last thing she had to do before she could go home, and it was taking forever. They really needed a computer upgrade.

"Another break-in?" Spencer's voice caught her off guard.

Nick looked up. Mr. Lawyer Dude was gone.

"Third one this month." Nick tried to sound cheerful, but all she wanted to do was throw the keyboard across the room. It was this kind of juvenile impulse that would keep her from getting promoted. Which worked for her - she liked being a detective. Who wanted to be a paper pusher, anyway?

"Those empty condos are easy targets," Nick sighed. There was a neighborhood of condos about seven miles away in their small town, and only half the condos were occupied.

Spencer nodded. He turned his old-school chair around, sitting on it backwards. Unlike the rest of the department, he insisted on sitting in the chair that did bad things to his back, just so he could turn it around and feel cool.

Nick rolled her eyes, but there was a smile on her face. "Are you sure you don't want to finish this for me?"

"And deny you the learning opportunity?" Spencer grinned. "Of course not."

Nick lobbed an eraser at him. "I have more years on the force than you do!"

"Not on this one." He picked up the eraser and tossed it back.

Spencer was a military veteran who had started his police career at the ripe old age of 35, fresh from a career he couldn't talk about. Spencer had been with the Battle Creek Police Department since he'd started. Nick had only been there three years. She had, however, been on the police force since she had graduated college at 21. Homicide detective in LA four years later, but... that hadn't gone how she'd expected. No one wanted to be a widow at twenty six.

The phone rang.

Nick sighed. It was her and Spencer up next for

whatever that call held. Dammit. She wasn't going to get home in time to take Lady Grey to the dog park. They'd have to go tomorrow. Besides, it was six in the evening, what could be that bad?

"Hello?" Nick picked up the phone and tucked it between the crook of her ear and shoulder.

"This is Officer Kennedy. We have a dead body found at one of the empty condos. Probable homicide." The patrol officer's voice faded into the background, and Nick sat up, gripping the phone tightly.

No.

Since Nick had been with Battle Creek Police, this was the first homicide that had landed in her lap. There was a reason she had moved away from LA.

She felt the phone plucked from her grasp.

The knock on the door. The police chief standing there, just looking at her.

That was when she knew her wife was dead.

She took a shaky breath, held it, then let it go. Over and over, until her breath came normally. Therapy had taught her something. She could hear Spencer's voice rumbling in the background.

Mentally she shook her head, dragging her attention back to the present. It wasn't her first homicide case, even if it was the first since Sarah's death. It wouldn't be her last, most likely. She just wasn't going to let herself get attached to anyone. She didn't want to see anyone she loved die in action any time soon.

Especially if she could have done something to prevent it.

"We'll be there soon." She heard Spencer set the phone back down, heard the soft click as he disconnected the call. The main calls came in via the land line, but all detectives had cell phones specifically for work. She touched her hip, felt the phone there.

Apprehension fluttered in her stomach, but she forced it away. "Where are we going?"

"North side," Spencer said, grabbing his jacket. "You're listed as the primary."

Nick's throat was dry. But then she nodded. She could do it.

"You okay?" Spencer stopped and looked at her. His steel-blue eyes were solemn.

Nick smiled, even though it was a sad one. "I can do it."

There was a flicker of relief in Spencer's face. "Good."

Nick rolled her eyes. "You don't have to parent me."

Spencer reached out and patted her shoulder. "I know." He turned and swept the office with his eyes.

Nick did the same thing, out of habit. Was she missing anything? A thrill went through her. Homicide scenes were different than anything else. With any luck, especially in a small town, they'd identify a suspect in the first forty eight hours. But not all cases were that simple.

"You're driving." Spencer dropped the keys in front of her.

"Aren't you supposed to be going home?" Nick looked at him, skeptical. If she was the primary, he didn't have to go.

"I like learning experiences." Spencer slipped his jacket on and headed out the door.

Shaking her head, Nick grabbed her suit jacket and followed him. Her heart was thudding loudly enough that she could have sworn it echoed in the empty department. She was dressed in black slacks, a white button-up shirt, and now a black blazer. Her gun and badge were on the belt around her hips. Detective to a T.

"How was the body found?" Nick glanced at Spencer out of the corner of her eyes as she drove.

"Anonymous 911 call," Spencer said grimly.

Nick sighed inwardly. She hated those. "Do they think it was the perp?"

"I doubt it," Spencer answered. "According to the 911 operator the voice was slurred, and came from a burner phone that wasn't at the scene. Sounds more like someone broke into the condo and found her than the perpetrator."

"You never know," Nick said.

Spencer nodded his agreement.

There were always so many unknowns with these cases. But it was something Nick loved.

"There." Spencer pointed to the crime scene tape. Nick pulled the police car up close to it, helping block the scene from the few civilians who had gathered around. It was dinnertime; why were they gathering like flies? Surely some of them had a life. She parked the car and turned it off.

Getting out of the car, Nick shut the door behind her and headed towards the tape. Spencer was a few steps behind her. "Sign here," a uniformed officer told her. He held out the log book. Nick quickly signed her badge number and her name, then her time entering. They kept a record of all who entered the crime scene and when. That way, if something happened, they would know who was there.

Nick accepted shoe covers from one of the crime-scene techs and then made her way inside. The condo was cookie-cutter, a typical bland two-bedroom home with a small driveway. The stark emptiness felt eerie. There were no pictures on the walls, no personal touches.

Turning past the hallway, Nick caught sight of the crime scene personnel and the crime scene itself. She steeled herself. It wasn't the worst she had seen, but homicide scenes were never enjoyable.

The crime scene investigators were working steadily, utilizing a grid system Nick had seen several times before. At the center of their grid was the body of a young woman, probably a few years younger than

Nick. She was covered in blood, her eyes still open and staring at nothing. There was blood spatter crawling up the walls, even some on the ceiling. Whomever the woman was, the attack had been personal.

Nick closed her eyes briefly, but she knew it was useless. Like many crime scenes before it, the image was now burned into her mind. By the time the case was solved, she would know its details better than her own life. "Walk me through it," she said, looking at the closest patrol officer.

The patrol officer was a young woman, maybe twenty four. She was dressed in full patrol uniform with the long sleeves of fall/winter. "I was sent to the scene by a dispatcher in response to an anonymous 911 call," she started. "Burner phone. Untraceable." The patrol officer grimaced.

Nick glanced at her name tag. Allison. "Thanks," she said. It confirmed what Spencer had told her, but it was always better to hear it from the source. Burner phones were the devil. Its use was a clue, though. This looked like a passion-motivated murder. Had the perpetrator called in out of guilt? Or was it someone else? And where did they get a burner phone?

"I found the victim already in rigor mortis," Allison continued as she led Nick inside. Both stopped for a moment. The medical examiner's office had arrived to get the body. Crime scene techs had already placed paper bags over her hands, and everything had been documented with photographs.

Being at the funeral, knowing that the one she loved was in that casket, never to wake up...

Nick wrenched herself back to the present. "What do we know so far?"

"There are signs of a scuffle." Allison pointed to the scruffy, run-down couch that seemed so out of place in the otherwise empty condo. There were specks of blood on the arm, and it was angled crookedly in the empty living room. "And of occupation. The fireplace has been recently used, and there are towels in the back bedroom that seem to have served as a crude bed."

"Need anything else?" The ME's assistant looked at Nick and Spencer.

Nick glanced at him, and he back at her, then Nick shook her head. "Document everything as usual, but the body can be released."

"I'll go with the body to make sure chain of custody is followed." Another patrol officer spoke up, one Nick recognized but she couldn't remember his name. The chain of custody of evidence was one of the most important things in criminal cases. Nick nodded, satisfied, and then turned back to Allison.

"Had anything been disturbed after the murder?" Nick glanced around the scene as the ME's assistant got to work.

"The body hasn't been moved. I'm guessing lividity

will confirm that." Allison searched the room with her eyes, as if she was thinking of anything else to say.

Nick looked at her, respect in her eyes. "You know a lot."

"My father was a detective," Allison said with a nod.

Nick jotted down notes. The autopsy would probably be tomorrow, and she would attend. That would tell her more. Lividity was what happened to a body after death. The blood would settle in the lowest part of the body in the position it was in. If someone moved it while the blood wasn't completely settled, the medical examiner could tell.

"What do you think?" Spencer asked.

Nick jumped; she had forgotten he was there. She exhaled slowly, taking a moment to gather her thoughts. "Someone squatting here would make the most logical sense with the recent break-ins, but this crime was personal." She glanced around at the blood spatter. That much blood was personal, not random. "A boyfriend, maybe, or a spurned lover?" Her gaze lingered on where the body was being placed in a body bag. "But why here? Where did she come from?"

"Questions, questions," Spencer agreed.

"We also need to find out how long this condo's been on the market." There might be a clue in that.

Spencer nodded. "I'll get one of the others to call in to the real estate company."

Nick tapped her lips with the top of her pen, briefly

lost in thought. There were a lot of questions to answer, there always were with a new case. But she would find the answers, and find whoever had killed the poor woman.

No matter what.

CHAPTER THREE

Tuesday, September 13th, 2016. 6:52pm.

Unease settled in Emma's stomach as she parked her car. She could see the commotion across the street, see the crime scene tape and the watchers. What was going on? At least it wasn't one of *her* condos. She grabbed her purse and slung it over her shoulder, then Emma's high heels clicked all the way up to the door of the small condo. She rang the doorbell, then waited.

Thirty seconds passed by and the unease deepened. She had an appointment with Julia at 7. Yes, she was a bit early, but that wasn't unusual.

She knocked, softly at first and then more desperately, ignoring the harsh grating of her knuckles against the wood of the door. Still no answer. No lights were on, either. She took a few steps back, glancing around for Julia's car. It was there. Where was Julia? Next step was breaking out her phone and dialing Julia's number.

She could hear the ringing inside the house. A shiver went down her spine. She pulled her keyring out of her pocket, searching for the master key.

Emma was the head therapist and owner of Belle's House, a safe shelter for domestic violence victims. Once they were getting back on their feet, they would move to one of the halfway homes, a series of condos they could use until they could afford their own place. It was a neighborhood composed of three separate condo settlements, and the condos were spread out to help preserve anonymity.

Part of Emma's job was to check on the women in the halfway house, and to continue their outpatient therapy as needed. It wasn't normal for them to miss an appointment. It wasn't normal for one of them to not be there. Not that they didn't miss things occasionally, but Julia had always been punctual.

In Emma's line of work, it didn't bode well.

She stood there for a moment, watching the scene out of the corner of her eye. A news crew had arrived and was setting up closer to her condo than the one sectioned off. They were close enough that Emma could hear them once the newswoman started speaking.

"A body has been discovered in an abandoned condo."

Emma's blood chilled to ice. It had to be a coincidence that she was looking for someone right across the street. Right?

There was a commotion closer to the door. Emma couldn't look away. A van labeled 'Clark County Medical Examiner' was parked close to the driveway, and two men dressed in dark blue jumpsuits with a medical logo wheeled a gurney out of the house.

There was a dark blue body bag on the gurney, and Emma's heart skipped a beat. Could it be? Was it Julia?

She had to know.

She stuck the keys back in her pocket and headed towards the crime scene tape, dodging the news crew and other assorted bystanders. Her heart was racing, her palms sweaty. There were patrol officers standing near the crime scene tape, and another one standing by the door.

Picking a spot between the two of them, Emma ducked under the tape and hesitated. Did she really want to go see? Did she want to confirm her worst fears, or should she save herself from the nightmare?

"Hey!" One of the patrol officers caught sight of her and headed her way. Emma ducked to the side, heading towards the ME's van. She had to know.

But the doors of the ME's van slammed closed before she could get there. Emma's heart plunged.

"Hello?" There was a new person, a woman about Emma's age, standing on the front step closest to Emma. She was dressed neatly, in a black blazer and slacks with a crisp white shirt. A gold badge glinted on her right hip, gun on her left. Her brown hair was short but stylish, and her dark blue eyes were sharp. She was staring straight at Emma.

Emma swallowed. Oh, shit. No matter the circumstances, the woman was gorgeous. Probably not something she was supposed to be thinking about, given the circumstances, but…

"Sorry." It was one of the patrol officers that spoke, the one standing right next to Emma. "She ducked under the tape and went after the ME."

"You shouldn't be here." She turned to the patrol officer. "Please escort—"

"I think I know who your victim is," Emma said before she could stop the words from leaving her mouth.

The gorgeous woman stopped mid-sentence, her eyebrows raised in surprise. "Excuse me?"

"I'm a therapist at Belle's House, a DV shelter. We have some women in halfway houses out here, and one of them isn't answering." The words came out in a rush, and there was more Emma could have said. Still, she couldn't help but hope it wasn't Julia. Maybe she had made a mistake.

"Maybe she's sleeping," the detective countered.

Emma shook her head. "They don't miss appointments. Not therapy." She paused. "And her car is here."

The woman pulled her blazer aside in order to grab the badge on her hip. "I'm Detective Nick Tanner. Call me Nick."

"Emma Stevens," Emma replied, taking her ID out of her purse and showing it to Detective Tanner. Nick took the ID from her, their fingers brushing. The hairs on Emma's neck prickled at the sizzle of electricity that passed between them.

Nope. She had no time for anything like that. Highly inappropriate.

"Where do you think this person lives?" Nick asked, glancing around the complex.

"There." Emma pointed across the street. "Her name is Julia." Present tense. Maybe Nick was right, and Julia had just gone out or something. The dread growing in Emma's middle didn't agree.

"And she's never done this before?" Nick pulled a notepad out of her pocket and jotted down something.

"No." Emma let out a slow breath. "I have a key to the apartment."

"What does she look like?" Nick lifted her head to meet Emma's eyes.

"Auburn hair, brown eyes. About five foot six, and she likes to wear sweatpants and a t-shirt around the house," Emma answered promptly. "She has a scar on her left arm, over the elbow."

Nick's writing stopped.

Emma swallowed thickly. "It's her, isn't it?"

Nick exhaled slowly. "The ME will have to confirm."

It was the answer Emma had been dreading.

A tall, salt-and-pepper-haired man came out of the house. "You go check that out," he told Nick.

"Eavesdropping again, Spencer?" Nick looked at him. She flipped the notebook closed and turned back to Emma. "Lead the way."

Emma nodded, feeling like water had been dumped over her in shock. She forced herself to keep it together, and headed back towards the crime scene tape. She ducked underneath it, Nick following, and immediately got accosted by the media.

"No comment," Nick said, nodding pleasantly to the man with the TV camera before steadily following Emma across the street.

"Sorry," Emma said, although she wasn't, really. She would have waded through an army of media to find out what had happened to Julia. Maybe her house would contain clues. Sliding the key into the lock, she twisted it to the side, hearing the door unlock.

"Is that her car?" Nick asked, looking over at the carport.

"Yes." Emma pushed the door open. It didn't help calm her nerves. On the small stand by the door were a wallet, keys, and phone. The screen of the phone showed just one missed call - Emma's number.

"Stay there." Nick followed her in, her hand on her gun. She was left-handed, Emma noted with random interest. Not that she was interested. She wasn't.

Technically Emma didn't ignore her when she moved a few steps further into the house. She stayed behind Nick, after all. But she caught sight of the crooked photos on the wall, the dining room table at an odd angle and the chair tipped over. Even the couch was crooked.

"Burglary?" Emma said before she could stop herself.

Nick looked back. Emma caught sight of her exasperation, but didn't let it bother her. "I doubt it." Nick bit her bottom lip lightly, seemingly lost in thought. "Do you have a photo of the resident?"

Emma turned back to the entrance, reaching for Julia's wallet.

"Stop!" Nick's voice was alarmed.

Emma froze.

"Sorry." Nick exhaled in a rush. "We shouldn't compromise the evidence."

Oh. "I don't have a photo." It was part of their security regimen. They kept as little identifying information as possible.

"Okay." Nick reached into her pocket and grabbed a pair of latex gloves, slipping them on and then gingerly picking up the wallet and opening it. It was very plain, nondescript. Dark in color, and when she opened it the insides were a lighter grey.

Emma watched as Nick pulled out a driver's license, her face grim. She could see the recognition in Nick's eyes. "It's her?"

Nick nodded once. "Do you know her next of kin?"

Emma shook her head. "We're the closest thing to kin she has," she said ruefully. "Julia never talked about her family."

"Do you know anything about them? Gather any info?"

Again, Emma shook her head. "We ask, but they can choose not to answer any questions. And even if they do answer, we can't guarantee that they are truthful." A lot of the women were being hunted, or had escaped bad situations. They didn't want to make it worse by forcing them to identify everyone. "I can get you the file I have on her back at the house."

Nick nodded once, seemingly distracted now. "Follow me."

Emma did. It was probably in her best interests. If she listened to Nick, built a rapport, maybe Nick would keep her updated on how the investigation was going. Julia was Emma's responsibility. If someone had taken her, and/or killed her, under Emma's nose - she was going to stop at nothing to find out who it was.

Nick led her back across the street to the salt-and-pepper man who was still standing in the doorway. "Spencer, we have a problem."

Emma blinked, then relaxed. Spencer was his name, most likely. At least it wasn't Houston.

"Yes?" Spencer looked at her, expectant.

"We have an ID on the victim," Nick said, her voice low.

Emma was surprised to hear a faint quiver. Emotion - sadness. Was she affected by Julia's death? Emma hoped so.

"She lived in the condo across the street." Nick nodded her head in the right direction.

Spencer looked at the people in the road in front of the tape, and sighed. "I'll let the techs know. You work with the patrol officers to mark off that condo."

Nick nodded, then went inside.

Emma stood there, not entirely certain she wanted to go inside and see what it looked like. The body was gone, but the crime scene remained. Her hands balled into fists, the keys in her hand cutting into her skin.

"Hey."

Nick caught her off guard. When had she come back?

"What?" Emma looked at her, startled, but the grip on her keys relaxed.

"Breathe." There was a very faint, rueful sort of smile on Nick's face. Like she had been there, done that, and knew where Emma's mind was.

Emma took a deep breath in and then exhaled, feeling some of the tension ease from her shoulders.

"There you go." Nick's eyes were intense.

"What are the next steps?" Emma asked, meeting Nick's gaze. She wanted to find who had done this to Julia. She wanted to get justice for Julia and all the other victims who couldn't speak for themselves.

Oh God. She had to tell everyone at Belle's House. Good thing she didn't need anything at home. She practically lived at Belle's House, anyway.

Nick's eyes searched the area around them. "Crime scene techs will work on both scenes until all evidence is catalogued, then it will be processed. Spencer -" she paused. "The other detective and I will be in charge of canvassing this neighborhood. Once that's done, we'll start following up leads." Her lips twisted into a wry smile. "Sleep is optional."

Emma understood that. "I want to help."

"You'll need to go back to the station at some point. I'm guessing you went to the victim - Julia's," Nick corrected herself, "often?"

Emma nodded. "She's been there about three months. I come by at least once a week." Probably a lot more than she should have, but like Nick had said, sleep was optional.

"You'll need to give your prints so we can exclude them from the scene." Nick jotted down a note.

"They're on record with the state as part of my licensing."

"Oh." Nick looked pleased. "That'll make it easier."

Emma wasn't sure what to say. She hadn't been in this particular situation before. Sure, some of her women had gone missing - most often found with their abusers, broken or bloody. But still alive.

"Ready?" Spencer came back out the door, looking at Nick.

"I want to come with you," Emma jumped in.

Nick and Spencer exchanged glances. "Civilians aren't really involved."

"I know how to talk to the ladies from Belle's House," Emma argued. She could feel heat rising in her, anger prickle like goosebumps across her skin. "I want to be there when you talk to them."

Spencer looked at Nick. "Your call."

Nick studied Emma intently. Emma didn't flinch.

"Fine. You're to stay back, and only get involved if it's one of your clients."

"Done." It wasn't Emma didn't care about the other residents, it was that her ladies were her priority. She grabbed her phone, typing out a quick text to one of the other therapists, her second-in-command, Vicky.

Cancelling appointments. Will need to have a House Meeting later. She doubted she could give out Julia's name quite yet. Nick was sticking her neck out and allowing Emma on part of the investigation. The least Emma could do was respect her in return.

The fact that Nick was cute definitely helped things. Not that Emma had noticed. Nope.

"Let's go," Nick said.

Emma followed. She had to find out who killed Julia. And she would - no matter what.

CHAPTER FOUR

Tuesday, September 13th, 2016. 7:02pm.

"We're going to the right," Nick said with a nod. "Are there any homes Spencer needs to avoid on the left?"

Emma shook her head, her soft, curly hair bouncing with the motion. "No. Belle's House has six condos on the right side." Her dark green eyes were fiery, something Nick respected.

She knew what it was like to want to protect people, to find out what had happened to someone she was responsible for, or someone she loved. Sarah flashed through her mind. Sarah had been both – first her partner at work, then in life. Grief threatened to swamp her. How many women would experience what she had, finding out that someone she knew, someone she cared for, was dead?

Nick started off towards the first door on her agenda, not waiting for Emma to follow. Emma was slightly shorter than Nick, but not by much. Dark green eyes, curly brown hair, long legs covered in dark blue jeans. She wore a long-sleeved sweater, which was suitable for autumn in the Northwest.

"Is this one of yours?" Nick asked, turning to face Emma.

Emma shook her head.

"Stay here." Nick left her down at the driveway and walked the ten feet to the door. It was sort of pointless, given how small the condos were, but it at least made her feel like she was following protocol. The lights were off and there was no car in the driveway. Nick didn't even know if it was occupied. She knocked regardless, listening for any movement inside the house.

Nothing.

"Battle Creek Police, just here to ask a few questions." Nick kept her voice high enough to be heard, but hopefully not loud enough to alarm. Hopefully.

No answer.

"I don't think anyone's home," Emma said from the driveway.

Nick chuckled, agreeing with Emma's assessment. "Bit of an anticlimactic start, eh?"

Emma nodded, and there was a hint of a smile on her face. "Next one is part of Belle's House."

"You can lead, then." Nick walked back towards her, and they walked side-by-side to the next door. This time there was a car, a small, beaten-up Toyota of some sort. She could see a faint glow through the curtains covering the windows. The TV, maybe?

Emma stopped a few feet away from the entrance, turning to Nick. Her voice was low. "Rachel's been out of the House for about three months now. She stayed at Belle's House for the full nine months before leaving."

Nick nodded, mentally noting the info. Emma seemed so calm and collected, even in the face of one of her clients being dead. It was something Nick liked, and respected. There was a warmth there, a sturdiness that Nick appreciated. Maybe they could talk about it over coffee. Once the killer was caught.

"Battle Creek Police, just want to ask a few questions." Nick knocked on the door.

Emma rolled her eyes. Nick retorted by raising her eyebrows. She wouldn't stick out her tongue, that was far too juvenile.

The door swung open a few inches, just enough for Nick to see a flash of black hair and brown eyes. She could see the chain of the lock keeping the door from opening further.

"Rachel?" Emma's voice was warmer than it had been moments before. "It's Emma."

"And the police?" The door opened a tiny bit more, the chain straining.

"There's a detective with me," Emma said. "We just need to ask you a few questions about anything you may have heard or seen last night."

Nick didn't let her expression twitch as Emma invited herself into the investigation. Well, maybe that ship had already sailed. Emma wasn't the worst type of civilian that Nick had dealt with. "I'm Detective Nick Tanner, with the Battle Creek Police. May I come in?"

"Can I see your ID?" Rachel asked, her voice soft.

"Of course." Nick took her badge off her hip, handing it to Rachel through the crack in the door. She watched as Rachel flipped it open, studied it and then Nick.

Then Rachel handed it back. "What's this about?"

The eye Nick could see flicked between them.

Emma glanced at Nick, then back at Rachel. "You'll want to sit down," she said, and there was a sadness in her voice.

"Okay." Rachel's voice was quiet, then she closed the door. Nick heard the sound of the chain being unlocked, then the door opened all the way. Nick let Emma lead the way in, letting Rachel greet the person she knew first.

When she caught sight of Rachel, Nick had to hide the shock on her face. She couldn't have been older than nineteen. Definitely not old enough to drink. It had been so easy to paint a different picture in her mind. Someone older, more ragged. Not a teenager.

But that was her own stereotypical view. Putting this aside, Nick grabbed her notepad and pen.

Rachel's face was wary, and there was a hardness there. Nerves, probably, with a helping of defensiveness. Nick had seen it in DV victims before.

Emma went over to her and drew her into a hug. Rachel wrapped her arms around her, holding her briefly before letting go.

The vulnerability surprised her. Part of Nick wanted to find out who had hurt her and ensure that they were punished - but that wasn't her job. Not yet. She took a deep breath. "I would like to ask you some questions about last night and this morning." They wouldn't have an approximate time of death until the autopsy, so she wanted to cover the broadest spectrum that she could.

Rachel's eyes were constantly moving, from Emma to Nick to the wall and back. Rachel nodded.

"When did you go to bed last night?" Nick wrote Rachel's name at the top of a page. Was it even her real name? She didn't know.

"About ten pm." Rachel's voice grew stronger, as if she was more confident in what she was saying. "I watched TV by myself for a couple of hours. A forensics show was on," she explained to Emma.

Nick nodded, jotting this down. "Did you hear or see anything unusual last night?"

Rachel thought for a moment and then returned her gaze to Nick's. "I heard someone scream."

"Did you call 911?" Nick asked, jotting down a note.

Rachel shook her head, uneasy. "I didn't think it was unusual. I wasn't even sure I heard it, really..." Her voice trailed off.

Nick nodded and pretended to write something down, but her mind spun. Something was fishy. She didn't suspect Rachel was involved in the crime, but there was something off about her story and the way she was telling it. How could she hear a scream but not report it? Was it really that common?

"Did you get up when you heard it?" Emma asked, her voice gentle.

Rachel shook her head, and she was wringing her hands now. "I thought maybe I was dreaming."

Nick relaxed somewhat. Still, it wouldn't hurt to ask around. "Do you know when you might have heard it?"

Rachel's eyes shifted to the left, thinking. "Around midnight."

Nick noted that down. "Do you know Julia? Her condo isn't far from yours."

Rachel glanced at Emma, who nodded. "Yes. We moved around the same time."

"How long have you been in this residence?"

"Three months." Rachel confirmed what Emma had said before they came in.

"Is there anything else you need to ask?" Emma asked Nick. She had angled her body to be between Nick and Rachel, her body language protective.

Nick glanced at her, trying to not get ruffled at her words. She had a job to do, after all. Even though she knew Emma had good intentions, Nick wanted to find the bastard who had murdered Julia.

"What happened to her?" Rachel's words were quiet. As if she didn't want to know the answer to her own question.

Nick hesitated. Could they release that yet?

Emma shot her a glare, but reached out and put her hand on Rachel's knee. "She was found in an empty condo."

Rachel's brows knitted together.

"She was murdered." Nick hated breaking the news.

Rachel's eyes widened, shock flashing across her face. It was a genuine reaction. "What?"

"Were you friends?" Nick jotted a question mark by Rachel's name. There could be something there, there could not be. But something was niggling at her senses, and as a detective, she had long learned to trust her instincts.

Rachel shook her head. "We all knew each other, but she roomed with Melanie, not me." Rachel looked at Emma. "She's really gone?"

"Yeah." Emma's lips were set in a thin line. "You can move back to Belle's House, if you want to."

Rachel shook her head. "I want to stay here."

Nick jotted that down. Why? "I think that's all the questions I have for now," she said.

"If you want to get in touch with Rachel in the future, I can get you her number." Emma looked at Nick, a challenge in her eyes.

Nick nodded, choosing not to argue. "Thank you," Nick said to Rachel.

"Bye," Rachel said, her eyes still a bit too distant. Shock was setting in. Nick felt a pang of sympathy. Whether it was a dear loved one or someone you knew by proximity, death always hit people hard.

"Please let me know if you need anything," Emma said, hugging Rachel fiercely. "I'll be arranging a memorial at Belle's House in the next week."

Nick watched them hug, then walked to the door, followed by Emma and Rachel. She smiled briefly at Rachel, then opened the door and went out. Emma followed.

The door closed behind them, and Nick heard the noise of the locks sliding into place.

"She's so young," Nick murmured, unable to stop the words from coming out. Half distracted, she brushed some pet hair off of her blazer and slacks. Was that from Rachel's or somewhere else? It was so easy to lose track.

Emma let out a sigh. "I wish she was the youngest one we've had at the House."

Nick glanced at Emma, not sure what to say.

"Have you always worked here?" Emma asked, her focus on the sidewalk in front of them as they headed to the next condo.

Nick shook her head. "I spent my first five years in LA." Her throat was dry just thinking about it. Even after three years it still hurt.

"Why did you come here?" They were standing at the sidewalk at the base of the next driveway.

"I wanted a change," Nick said simply. She wasn't going to talk about what had happened with Sarah, not yet. Unconsciously she felt her thumb rub her ring finger, an echo of the ring that had been there until she had finally taken it off eighteen months ago. She saw Emma's eyes move and stopped the behavior, not wanting to get caught.

"Hm," Emma said instead. "Let's get going."

Three hours later, she and Emma had finished the rounds of the condo complex and were back at the intersection between Julia's place and the crime scene.

It was late now, the humidity being offset by the cool air. Nick was glad for the blazer.

"What next?" Emma looked at her.

Nick dragged her mind out of her to-do list, bringing it back up to the present.

"Can I tell the other ladies at Belle's House?"

Only the faintest quiver of Emma's lips betrayed

her thoughts about doing that. Nick's heart broke for her. It was never easy. "We need to notify next of kin first."

"We're the closest thing to next of kin that Julia has." Emma's voice was flat as she repeated what she had said earlier. Not defensive, but - personal, almost? It was something very close to Emma's heart.

Nick sighed. A few people had reported a dog barking (yet none of the residents owned a dog). One had reported a strange car lurking around, but only knew it was a dark color, not the make or model. Someone had even reported gunshots - but then followed that up with "it was the aliens", so Nick didn't give that whole testimony a lot of credit. Still, she had dutifully written it down.

"What'd you find out?" Spencer caught her off guard.

Nick looked up, seeing him and a couple of the patrol officers heading their way. "Most commonly reported is a dog barking and strange car in the area, although we've also heard reports of a gunshot and a scream." She could recall them from memory, but she also had notes to return to. It wasn't easy to remember every detail of a case, especially if they dragged on.

Hopefully this one wouldn't, but Nick wasn't feeling particularly optimistic with what they learned.

"Sounds about right. We can compare notes at the

station." Spencer turned to look at Emma. Emma raised her chin slightly, meeting his gaze with her own. Spencer made a thoughtful noise and then turned back to Nick.

"Is there anything else you need?" Emma turned to look at Nick.

"We'll need to come by and talk to your ladies at some point," Nick said, exchanging looks with Spencer.

"They'll respond best to a female detective." Emma looked between the two of them.

Spencer chuckled. "Guess that'll be you then, Nick."

"Apparently." Nick wasn't really surprised. "Where can I find Belle's House?"

Emma shook her head, then reached out her hands for Nick's pen and paper. "The address is secret. Call me when you're ready to come, and I'll give it out."

Nick gave her the pen and paper. It was probably one of the more convenient ways to get a cute girl's number.

Not that Nick was really interested in her. Nope. She wasn't going to go down that road. Sarah's bright smile flashed through her mind and guilt melded with fear to settle low in her stomach. How could she replace Sarah? She couldn't. It wasn't a loss she wanted to risk ever again.

"Would tomorrow morning work?" Nick asked.

Emma nodded.

Nick was already running through her to-do list in

her mind. She needed to check on how the evidence was doing, try and find Julia's next of kin, consult with Spencer. Her to-do list was miles long, with no sleep on the horizon.

But if that was what it took to find a killer, it was what Nick would do.

CHAPTER FIVE

Tuesday, September 13th, 2016. 11:23pm.

Ignoring traffic laws, Emma dialed her phone the moment she got into her car. Her car wasn't new enough to have one of those fancy Bluetooth phone things, so she turned her phone on speaker and tucked it into the steering wheel. Improvisation.

"Hello?" Vicky, one of the other therapists and her second-in-command, answered promptly. With all the chaos, Emma wasn't certain who was working the night shift.

Relief washed through Emma. "Hey, Vicky," she said, her voice soft. "We need to have a House Meeting."

"What happened?"

"Do you remember Julia?" Emma didn't want to

give the news over the phone, but Vicky needed to know that it wasn't good.

"Of course." Although Emma had been Julia's primary therapist, the therapists covered for each other on a rotating basis, and some led group therapy. They knew all of the girls.

"She was murdered." The words hung in the air, although Emma's attention was on the road in front of her.

"I'll call in the on-call therapists," Vicky said, her voice grim. "Meeting in thirty minutes."

"Sounds good." The on-call therapists would go get the halfway house women. Thirty minutes was enough for them to drive the women who were awake back to the house, and if they couldn't make it, Emma or Vicky could go talk to them later. She doubted this would be the last meeting they would have about what had happened.

Emma disconnected the call and tossed her phone onto the passenger seat. The drive back to Belle's House was rural, mostly back roads and occasionally no roads at all. But it was worth it for the privacy it gave them.

Emma had inherited Belle's House from her mother. It was where she had grown up, where she had lived with her sometimes-father when he bothered to show up. Emma had gotten a good look at the effects of domestic violence close-up. Her mother had loved him until she died. It was enough to make Emma swear off any relationship, no matter the gender.

Her phone buzzed, but she ignored it. She could look when she parked.

Belle's House came into view. It was old-looking, almost Victorian, but Emma had renovated the inside. There were also the security measures that people couldn't see. Hidden in the trees were security cameras, so the security guards could monitor car arrivals and check whether or not their license plates were on the approved list. They did everything they could to keep Belle's House a secret.

The last thing they wanted was for a spurned husband to find Belle's House in the middle of the night and take revenge on whomever he felt had wronged him. Sometimes that was his partner, sometimes it was the staff.

Emma pulled her car up towards the front of the driveway, turning it off as soon as she parked. She was dreading the responsibility she had to fulfill, but it was hers and hers alone. Belle's House had only been up and running for five years. This was their first death.

Emma let out a deep breath and headed towards the front door. Unlike normal homes, this led her into a small foyer-like area that had a security guard sitting at a desk, monitoring the cameras.

"Can I see your ID, Miss Stevens?" Like the rest of the staff, the security guard was a woman. No matter that Emma owned the place, she went through the same protocols as everyone else.

"Here." Emma pulled out her ID to show her and then stopped. There was a business card on top of it.

Detective Nick Tanner. Then a number.

Emma hummed. Interesting. She tucked the business card in her pocket and presented her ID, as asked.

Then Vicky appeared in the doorway, her face both neutral and sad at the same time. "We're assembled. Most of the halfway ladies are here, too."

Emma's stomach plummeted. It wasn't the time to be thinking about anything other than her duty to the women in her protection. "Let's go."

When she made it to the common area, there were about fifteen women spread in a rough half-circle, some sitting and the others standing. They took up three couches, two chairs, and the floor. Despite the pain of the current situation, Emma couldn't help a faint smile. This was what she had worked so hard for. Saving women's lives, helping them find the worth in themselves.

She moved to stand at the head of the room. All eyes were on her, even the non-residents. Four therapists were there, spread roughly throughout the room. Vicky nodded when she caught Emma's eye - she had warned them what was coming.

"Last night, Julia was murdered," Emma said, her

voice as soft as she could make it to ease the blow. Not that it helped.

Some women gasped, some didn't move at all. Being victims of domestic violence, the women's reaction to grief was often unexpected compared to those of 'normal' people. But Emma knew that everyone was hurt by it, whether they showed it or not.

"Do they know who did it?" Rachel was the one who spoke up. She was sitting near the edge, as was her habit. She was next to Gemma, her former roommate and another one of the Halfway House ladies. While the Halfway House ladies were dressed, most of the residents were in their pajamas.

"Not yet," Emma answered calmly. "But I can assure you, the police are working on it and there's a good team searching for her killer."

Another hand shot up.

"Yes?" Emma looked at Melanie. She was Julia's former roommate, and the one Emma was worried about the most.

"What happened?" Melanie's voice shook.

It was the question Emma had been dreading most. "We don't know," she answered honestly. "I'll share more details as I hear them."

"Are you working with law enforcement?" Gemma asked.

"Yes." Emma thought of Nick, then shoved her out of her mind. "I'm working with one of the detectives to ensure that Belle's House is kept safe during the course of this investigation."

That seemed to relax some of the women. The air was heavy with grief, but there was a reassurance, too. Belle's House was their safe haven. The murder would have been that much more distressing had it happened there.

Emma sent up a brief prayer. *Please let there be no murders in Belle's House.*

"There will be a female detective here tomorrow to interview all of you about Julia," Emma continued. "I hope you will all co-operate to the best of your abilities." She knew it wouldn't be easy for all of them - domestic violence victims and police didn't always go hand in hand. "But I'll be there if you would like me to be."

The questions came fast and furious after that. When would the memorial be, where would she be buried, had they found Julia's family? They were questions that Emma didn't know the answer to.

"I'd like to talk to the Halfway House women for a minute." Emma pitched her voice high enough that it carried across the crowd.

"Use the kitchen," Vicky advised. "Tilly's making treats."

Mentally, Emma fist-pumped. Pastries would make everything better. The wave of shame caught her off guard; how could she be happy about something like that when one of her ladies had been murdered?

Of course, she could hear the voice of one of her therapy professors from school.

Everyone handles grief differently.

But not everyone was the model for a house of women dealing with a loss. It was different when it was personal.

Rachel, Gemma, and the others followed Emma into the kitchen. They gathered around the countertop island, which had three trays of pastries on it. Emma looked at them, mesmerized for a moment. Should she eat one? Should she not? Was it bad if she did?

She had to be an example. Picking up an apple turnover, she bit into it, savoring the sweetness of the pastry combined with the tartness of the apple. She hadn't eaten much that day, which often happened when she was making rounds, and the turnover warmed her stomach.

Hesitantly, then with more confidence, each of the women picked up a pastry of their own. Once Emma finished her mouthful, she sat the turnover down on a paper towel. "I understand that some of you may be alarmed after what happened to Julia," she said, her voice calm. Inside she was a maelstrom, but she had to keep it together for them. If she freaked out, so would everyone else. "If you wish to return to the shelter of Belle's House, we will make arrangements for you. It might be cramped, but we will accommodate all of you in a secure location."

The last thing she wanted was for another one of her ladies to get hurt. Maybe it was just a one-time thing. A murder of passion. Maybe no one else would be hurt. But she wasn't willing to take the chance.

"I want to come back," Gemma said. Three of the other ladies agreed. Maria, Sandy and Irene.

Emma looked at the others. There were two. "You're okay staying in your condos?"

Rachel was the first to nod. Then Tansy. "Yes."

"Alright. Do you have any more questions?" Emma looked around, meeting the eyes of each of the women.

"Will there be a funeral?" Rachel asked.

"They're looking for next of kin. Regardless, we'll have a ceremony here in the next week." Emma's throat began to clog, and tears threatened to come to her eyes. She needed to take a break from all of this, get herself back under control. She forced the emotions back. She couldn't break down. There would be time for emotions later.

"Let me know if you need anything else," Emma told them. They all had her number, and she carried her phone with her at all times. Work/life balance wasn't for someone like her.

The women nodded, and Emma left the room. She caught Vicky's attention and headed towards the entrance. She stopped by the living area, where the women had gathered, and took a moment to check on them. Melanie had left, so had one or two other women. The air in the room was reserved, sad but resilient.

What did she do now? The women had their therapists, as needed. She could stay and provide therapy, but that was why she had staff – for situations no one expected.

It was nearing midnight. Sleep made the most sense. She couldn't go back to the police department to give her statement or find anything else out until the morning, until Nick called her.

"Call me if you need me," she said, her hand on Vicky's arm. "I'll be upstairs."

Vicky nodded, but didn't speak.

Emma could see the tears at the corner of her eyes. At least Emma knew she wasn't the only one who was struggling to keep it all together.

Swallowing back her emotions, Emma nodded once, firmly. "Later."

She headed upstairs to her office that often doubled as a bedroom when she had too much work to do. Her office was on the top floor, near the front of the building. They kept blinds on all windows, but there were enough gaps between the slats that she could look out and see their surroundings.

The part of the cleared-out forest that served as a parking lot was empty outside, except for the few cars of the employees and the ladies who had them. Tall evergreen trees surrounded the house, the pine needles covering the forest floor. She couldn't smell the air, but she knew how it smelled. Good and fresh, something that made her feel a bit better, even in the midst of what was happening. She closed her eyes, feeling some of the tension seep from her shoulders. Maybe Detective Tanner had made progress. Maybe she had identified the killer.

It probably wasn't a good idea to go see the attractive detective again, any more than she had to. Detective Tanner's self-assurance was enticing, and the way she had been so gentle when talking with the women from Belle's House was something Emma appreciated.

A wave of emotions hit her like a tsunami. She leaned forward, her head in her hands and her heart racing. She closed her eyes, fighting back the tears. She wasn't going to cry. She was stronger than that.

It was so hard to lose someone who she'd cared for, who she'd looked after. Who she'd been responsible for.

She shoved the feelings back down. She couldn't break down now, not when she had things to do. Once the police had caught Julia's killer, then she could allow herself to cry and grieve. For now, she just had to push forward.

She picked up Nick's card, looked at it and the number. Part of her wanted to hear Nick's voice, to be reassured. Hear the determination in her voice and know with absolute conviction that she would catch the killer. But that was silly.

So instead, she settled on sending Nick Julia's case file, with all the information they had. That would have to do.

CHAPTER SIX

Wednesday, September 14th, 2016. 7:02am.

Nick sat in her desk chair, her feet up on the orthopedic thing. As annoying as it was, it did provide good thinking posture. Especially after she'd only grabbed four hours of sleep on the cot in the interrogation room.

"Any luck on next of kin?" Spencer asked, his desk next to hers.

"Nope." Nick grimaced. Emma had sent over all the information she had on Julia, but it wasn't much. Since the women were often fleeing from someone, they didn't give a ton of information. And even within those constraints, Julia had given very little.

At least her name seemed to be real. All she could find in the public records were her parents, and they were both dead. The birthdays matched up with what

Julia had given Emma during intake, but there were no leads on more distant relatives. Maybe Emma had been right, and Belle's House was the closest kin she had.

"No luck on identifying who sent her to Belle's House, either." Spencer frowned. "She worked at the diner across the street from the courthouse. I'm heading there later to talk with the owner and her co-workers."

"I guess that means I get the interviews at Belle's House?" Nick said ruefully.

Spencer raised his eyebrows, his face spelling out "duh". "You're a girl."

"A woman," Nick corrected, shooting a glare at him.

Spencer grinned, pleased his teasing had gotten to her. "Same thing."

Nick rolled her eyes. While she had encountered some misogyny in her rise up the ranks, Spencer was pretty harmless. He just liked getting under her skin. Like a sibling.

"The autopsy is scheduled for this afternoon," Spencer said, reading one of the files in front of him. "I'd like you to attend if you can."

"Yup." It was standard procedure to go to the autopsy, especially in a case like this, where clues from the autopsy could help direct their investigation.

"If you can drag yourself away from that cute thera-pist." Spencer kept his face straight.

Nick looked up, but didn't look at him. "I wasn't staring at her."

"Mhm." Spencer nodded.

"Shit." Was she? She hadn't noticed anything.

"Now you will be." Spencer smiled at her, then turned back to his file.

Nick contemplated throwing a paperclip at his head, but decided to ignore him instead. Emma *was* cute.

Dragging her mind away from how cute Emma was, Nick flipped to a new page in her notebook and made a list. Emma's name was first, with a question mark there. Not just due to her cute status, but she was involved in a lot of the different facets of the case. Maybe she knew more than she thought, things that weren't included in the files she had sent over. Nick wanted to know where she fit into all of this.

Then there was Rachel. None of the other residents had mentioned a scream, not even Spencer's interviews. Was she lying, or had she been the only one close enough to hear the scream? Nick was skeptical. She wanted to talk to Rachel again. If she was lying, there was a reason. If she wasn't, that still needed to be looked into.

Nick's phone rang, drawing her attention. She grabbed her cell out of her pocket, answered it and tucked it to her ear. "Detective Tanner."

"It's Emma Stevens." Emma's voice rang in her ear.

Nick put down the file she had been looking at, suddenly interested. "How may I help you?"

"I wanted to let you know that there's time to do the interviews this morning around nine, if you want to drop by." There was urgency in Emma's voice, the same hope that Nick felt. If they intensified their efforts now, did as much as they could in the first forty-eight hours, there was a higher chance that they would catch who did this. The person who had killed Julia.

"I'll be there in twenty." Nick went to hang up, then stopped. "Uh. What's the address?"

There was a faint laugh in Emma's voice as she rattled off the address. "It's a bumpy drive."

Nick glanced out of the window at her police cruiser. That was going to be fun. "I'll be there soon." She turned to Spencer, opened her mouth to speak, and was cut off with a wave.

"Go have fun," Spencer said, then his face turned serious. "Bring us back the information we need to solve this case."

Nick nodded. "I'll do my best."

IT WAS nine on the dot when Nick arrived at Belle's House. She hadn't gotten lost, and was thankful for small mercies. There were a couple of cars in the scattered driveway. One had a person in it.

She turned the lights and sound off, not wanting to alert anyone to her presence. Putting a hand on the holster of her gun, she carefully got out of the car, trying not to make a sound.

The police cruiser's door creaked, something that made Nick sigh inside. Of course it did. The lights of the other car turned on. Nick froze.

"Detective Tanner?" It was Emma's voice, and Emma who got out of the car.

"Oh." Nick didn't realize she had said that out loud until Emma laughed. "Yeah, it's me."

Emma just nodded, the movement of her head faintly visible in the silhouette of her car's lights.

"Do you ever sleep?" Nick asked. She had a feeling that Emma was a workaholic, just like her.

Suddenly guilt stabbed at Nick's heart. Lady Grey. She'd completely forgotten about her. God, she was the worst dog parent ever.

She grabbed her phone, typing out a quick request to Jordan. Hopefully she and Carys would be able to check on her and make sure she was okay. In return, Nick would owe them dinner. Or something.

"Sorry." Nick tucked her phone away, confident (hopefully) that Lady Grey would be taken care of.

It buzzed almost immediately, and she pulled it out in surprise.

She's been here since last night. Spencer tipped us off.

Nick felt a wave of gratitude for friends who took

care of things even when she didn't. At least she knew her dog was safe and happy.

Emma nodded in acknowledgement. "I'll sleep when I'm dead," she said.

Nick blinked, and it took her a moment to realize that Emma was answering her previous question. Then she grinned. "Me, too."

The corner of Emma's lips turned into a smile, something that sent annoyingly giddy butterflies through Nick's stomach. Shut that down, right now, she chastised herself. Nope, nope, nope.

"You were asleep in the car, weren't you?" Nick took a stab in the dark.

Emma grinned, letting out a soft laugh. "I was getting coffee." She raised the two large cups. "Gotta keep going."

Nick had been there more than once or twice. "Lead the way."

Emma did. They entered through the front door, which revealed a small foyer instead of the warm entranceway Nick had expected. "You need to sign in with security," Emma said, pointing to the desk. "You also need to sign these forms - to swear you'll preserve the anonymity of Belle's House and its location." Emma grabbed some forms off the desk, along with a pen, and pushed them in Nick's direction. "We will also need a photocopy of your badge," she added.

Nick took the papers and started filling them out,

her handwriting smooth and even. It was something she got teased for at the police department. Police officers were supposed to have chicken scratch, weren't they?

"Are you comfortable handing your badge over?" Emma asked.

Nick unclipped it from her waistband, passing it to Emma. She trusted Emma, as stupid as that was. She was a police officer, a detective. Trusting someone when there wasn't any firm evidence saying she could was dangerous. But she did. She watched as Emma took a copy of it and then handed it back, and it went straight back onto Nick's belt.

Once the paperwork was done, Emma copied that, too. It should have been strange, standing there, watching her do essentially secretarial work, but it wasn't. Instead, Nick felt comfortable around her, even with the female security guard sitting there watching them.

"Anything else?" Nick asked, her posture relaxed with a thumb in her pocket. Belle's House was strange to her, but it felt like home. That was probably deliberate, too, given the nature of the women that lived there.

"Not at the moment." There was a ragged smile on Emma's face, which quickly disappeared. "Follow me."

Nick took a deep breath. She had done hundreds of interviews before, these wouldn't be that different. But they were, because Emma would be watching.

"We have security and cameras on twenty-four seven," Emma said, her voice low. She was taking Nick through some of the back passageways, apparently. "There are therapists on staff at all times, although most of the appointments are during the day. The women and staff work together to keep the place clean, and to cook meals that are eaten as a group in the living area."

"How many women are here?" Nick asked. She wasn't entirely certain if she would have to interview all of them, but when in doubt, more interviews were better than less. Maybe Spencer would find something at the diner.

"Thirteen right now," Emma said. "We're a bit over capacity due to some coming back from the halfway houses."

Nick could understand that. Why stay in an unsecured halfway home when you could come back to the security of Belle's House, and enjoy the companionship of the other residents? "I'd like to start by interviewing Julia's former roommate."

"Melanie is her name," Emma said, giving Nick a short nod. "I already notified her that you were coming. You can use one of the therapy rooms."

"Are you sitting in?"

Emma looked at her. "Yes."

Yeah that was about what Nick expected. She simply nodded. Pulling her notepad out of her breast pocket, she followed Emma into one of the rooms. It was small, like a bedroom, with a couch on the far side, a desk opposite it, and two plush chairs facing the couch. Where to sit, where to sit.

She settled on one of the plush chairs, shifting until she was comfortable. She kept her notepad closed on the arm of the chair. She wouldn't use it unless absolutely necessary. Sometimes note-taking made people uncomfortable.

"I'll go get Melanie." Emma left the room without a backwards glance, leaving Nick alone with her thoughts.

Her phone buzzed and she looked down at it. Jordan had sent her an image.

A smile came to Nick's face. It was Lady Grey, her front paws down in a play bow, getting ready to race across the room chasing after whatever had caught her interest. Nick didn't have kids, and didn't plan to. Lady Grey was her child.

There was a soft knock on the door and Nick hastily tucked her phone away, turning to face the door. Then it opened. A small, blonde-haired woman entered, with Emma right behind her. The woman - presumably Melanie - was dressed in jeans with a t-shirt and sandals that seemed out of place for the rainy weather. But Belle's House was kept warm, so maybe it didn't matter.

Nick stood, extending her hand for Melanie to

shake. "I'm Detective Tanner," she said. "You can call me Nick." More casual titles helped some people feel more comfortable around her.

"Melanie," the small blonde woman said. She settled on the couch, Emma taking the other side but close enough for Melanie to reach as needed.

"I understand that you and Julia were roommates?" Nick kept her voice as gentle as she could. She could only imagine what the poor woman was going through.

Melanie nodded. "I've been here about seven months. Julia left a couple of months ago. We lived together until then."

Emma nodded in confirmation.

"Do you mind if I take notes?" Nick asked. When Melanie shook her head, Nick wrote her name at the top of the page. "When was the last time you saw Julia?" She wasn't sure how often the women were allowed to leave the house.

"We had a potluck last week," Melanie said. "She came by." She glanced at Emma. "The week before, I went over to her place for lunch. Vicky took me."

"One of the therapists," Emma clarified.

Nick nodded, jotting down notes. "Did Vicky work with Julia, too?" This question was for Emma.

Emma shook her head. "Julia was one of my clients. Melanie worked with Vicky."

Melanie nodded in agreement.

"Did you two talk often?" Maybe Melanie could help her with Julia's last movements.

Melanie nodded. "At least once a day."

"When was the last time you talked?" This could help them figure out when Julia had been taken from her condo.

"She went to bed around 9pm," Melanie said, her face thoughtful. "It was a normal day. She didn't mention anything abnormal."

Nick jotted notes down as Melanie kept talking. Julia sounded like she had a normal routine pretty well established. That was good, it would make their lives easier.

"Do you know if Julia was involved with anyone?" Nick looked at Melanie, her voice as compassionate as she could make it.

Melanie tilted her head back, looking at the ceiling. Then she nodded.

Nick tried to keep the interest off her face. She had to stay professional. "Do you remember a name?"

"I don't know who she was dating before she came here," Melanie said, her eyes distant, "but she used to talk about a Ryan. I think he works as a bartender at one of the local bars, The Dive."

Nick jotted this down, adrenaline flowing through her veins. It was their first proper lead. "What did she used to say about him?"

Melanie looked down at her clasped hands. "He used to beat her," she said, her voice quiet.

"Did she come here because of him?" Nick glanced at Emma, then back to Melanie.

"I don't know." Melanie shrugged. Tears were starting to gather in the corner of her eyes, and Emma wrapped an arm around her shoulders.

Emma looked at Nick.

"I don't have any more questions right now," Nick said.

Melanie nodded, her hands coming up to rub her eyes. She sniffled. Emma reached over and grabbed a tissue for her.

Nick's heart broke for the women in front of her. Melanie had lost a friend - a good one, by the sound of it - and Emma had lost someone she considered herself in charge of. Someone she cared for. Yet there Emma was, soldiering on. Doing everything she could to prevent that from happening to someone else.

But they had a lead, finally.

"You don't have to stay," Emma said to Melanie.

Nick nodded. Melanie grabbed another tissue and left the room.

"Do you want to interview any of the others? Or do you want to follow up on this Ryan?" Emma's gaze was intense.

Nick weighed the pros and cons. She needed to talk to Spencer. "I need to make a phone call."

Emma nodded. "I'll be right back."

Nick dialed Spencer on her cell, listening to it ring. "Hello?"

Nick could hear the echo of people in the background. Maybe he was still at the diner. "I got a lead on a potential ex for Julia," she said.

"Have you talked to all the ladies there?" Spencer asked.

"Not yet. Do you want me to pursue the lead or finish the interviews?" Nick leaned back on the couch, aware of some movement just outside the door. Was this Emma's office? It was. She could see a picture of Emma on the desk. She looked a bit younger, was smiling and holding keys. Was that when she opened Belle's House, maybe?

"Autopsy's in a couple hours, so let's go get his story now so we'll know if it matches. Want to meet me at the bar?"

"Sounds good. I can finish the interviews up later. Get anything from the diner?" Nick asked. She closed her notepad and tucked it and the pen into the left breast side pocket. It was more secure that way, more hidden.

"Nothing." Spencer sounded grim. "No reports of a boyfriend, no one she paid special attention to. She kept her eyes on her work, smiled, and did what she had to do."

Nick let out a sigh. "Go figure."

CHAPTER SEVEN

Wednesday, September 14th, 2016. 1:34pm.

The trip to the bar proved fruitless - Ryan was off schedule, they didn't have an address and he wouldn't be back until later that night. Spencer touched her shoulder, jolting her out of her brief nap. Nick yawned and stretched, looking around the interrogation room she was sleeping in out of habit. Nothing had changed since she had closed her eyes. "Thanks."

She rubbed the sleep out of her eyes, sitting up and adjusting her white blouse. No way was she going to get all of the wrinkles out. Good thing she had another one. Her blazer was hanging on one of the chairs.

"Autopsy time, then picking up Ryan for a polite chat." Spencer smiled, but there was an edge to it. He wanted to find their murderer as much as she did. "Ready to head to the ME's office?"

"Walking or driving?" Nick stifled another yawn, digging her extra set of clothes out of her overnight bag.

"Up to you."

"Walking," Nick decided. "It'll wake me up some."

"We have to get to the bar by six to talk to Ryan," Spencer said.

"Yup." Nick dug into the breast pocket of her blazer, grabbing the notebook. Later she wanted to make a whiteboard, start making a list of the people they had talked to and who they still needed to trace. That way she could see the full picture.

She ducked into the bathroom and changed clothes. There was a definite advantage to having short hair - it didn't take much to make it presentable. Spencer was standing by the door when she got out, his arms crossed over his chest. Mostly patient.

"Let's go." Nick pushed open the main doors of the department, Spencer not far behind. Nick's mind was drifting, reviewing what they knew so far. The autopsy would give them more clues and hopefully give them a time frame for when the death had occurred.

While Nick and Spencer worked for Battle Creek's police department, they were close to where Clark County had all of its county resources, including the Medical Examiner and the courthouse. The ME's office was on the farthest side, a short, nondescript building that hid its true purpose.

Signing in at the desk, Spencer and Nick headed through the first set of doors. They opened up into the larger autopsy room with five stainless steel autopsy tables. She could see a few offices to the side, full of files and cabinets. Lights shone down on the steel autopsy tables, and Nick caught sight of the drains on the floor. She wasn't one of those who fainted at the ME's office, but it wasn't something she particularly enjoyed, either.

One of the tables was already occupied, the body of the young woman - Julia's body - stretched out on it, everything but her head covered with a thin sheet. Apparently the ME had finished the external exam and had removed her clothes, leaving her covered with the sheet until Nick and Spencer arrived.

The medical examiner in question, a man in his mid-30s named Evan, stood over the table, obviously in the middle of something.

It was always strange, seeing the medical examiners and their assistants. They looked almost like aliens, dressed in their blue coverings and face shields. Their work could get bloody.

"What do we know so far?" Nick asked Evan.

"Death was caused by blunt force trauma," Evan said, his voice low and melodious. There was a lilt to it, a dry sort of humor that made listening to his autopsy results less horrifying. "I also found a welt on her arm."

"A beating?" Nick was already jotting down notes.

"Yes, but not on her arm." Evan turned Julia's arm over, pointing out the purple-and-blue splotch and the spidery veins fleeing from it. "Some type of injection. Won't know what it is until I do the internal exams and get the toxicology back."

"Some type of drug?" Nick asked. If she had been drugged, maybe that was how the perpetrator had got her from her home to the empty condo. Or maybe that was how she'd ended up in the empty condo in the first case. Was it drug-related? She made a note to ask Emma.

Evan shrugged. "We won't have toxicology back for a few weeks, but if you ask me, someone injected her with a drug that shouldn't have been injected."

Street drugs came in all different shapes and sizes. "Something illegal?"

Evan chuckled. "Do you see the toxicology reports?"

The corner of Nick's lips tugged up into a faint smile. "Best guess?"

"Pill crushed when it shouldn't be. I've seen it in a few overdose cases before. It does nasty stuff to the veins." Evan was preparing for the internal examination now, the sheet folded back and tucked somewhere else. Nick kept her eyes on the ME, trying to respect the dead woman's privacy.

Interesting. Nick hadn't seen or heard of any drugs in Julia's condo, or seen any mention of them in Emma's case file. Had the drugs been brought by the killer? Those would take some time to prepare, and require some knowledge. Would that be something Ryan would know how to do?

"So you're thinking she was drugged before she was killed?" Spencer asked, tapping his fingers on his chin as he thought.

"Probably." Evan lifted up Julia's shoulder slightly, showing the faint red marks underneath the blood spatter. "These are drag marks from a carpet, most likely." He showed them the arm again. "And her blood was definitely flowing when it was injected."

"The condo she was found in is all hardwood," Nick mused.

"Wherever she was, she came into contact with a carpet or something similar." Evan laid her back down gently. "I'll be able to tell you more when this is done."

Nick took a deep breath before she looked at Julia's - the victim's - head. Blunt force trauma victims weren't pretty, not in death. Blood matted her hair, and there were dents in her skull. Whatever it was, whoever had done that, it had been serious overkill.

A passion-based crime, then? Although this assumption had been obvious from the beginning, Ryan would make sense. Any previous partner needed to be investigated.

Spencer's phone rang and he took a few steps away, answering it.

Nick turned her attention back to Julia lying on the

table. Her face was serene in death, even with the blood all over her face.

Spencer came back, excitement flashing over his face. "County police caught Ryan speeding in Portland. He was trying to flee."

"Well, I think it's time for us to go." A grin crossed Nick's face. That was a good sign, someone fleeing after a murder. Especially when Julia's name hadn't been announced to the press yet.

Guilt tugged briefly at her heartstrings. Next of kin. They still hadn't found anyone who cared about her, besides the ladies at Belle's House.

"Patrol officers are bringing him to our department to enjoy the hospitality," Spencer said. They bade their farewell to Evan and his assistant, signed out, and started the walk back to the station.

By the time they got there, one of the patrol cars was arriving with a scruffy-looking white guy in his mid-20s. Was that Ryan? Most likely.

He was handcuffed, and one of the patrol officers helped him out of the car. The charge of evading arrest was useful. Something they could drop if necessary to get him to co-operate.

Nick and Spencer headed into the station. The interrogation rooms were modern, set up with mandatory recorders for both visual and audio. It wasn't perfect, but it worked. Nick grabbed a proper notepad, large enough she could write anything she needed to.

Spencer collected the case file and all the notes they had on the case so far. They didn't have a time frame yet, so getting Ryan to detail his whereabouts the whole day and night was important.

They headed to the interrogation room where Ryan was. Room B. It was dimly lit, with a single light fixture hanging above their heads and a cheap table bolted to the floor. There were two chairs on each side. The chairs were also bolted to the floor. Just in case.

Nick went over and took the cuffs off. Until they had more proof of wrongdoing, it didn't make sense to keep him in handcuffs. Not when they wanted to build good will and get him to talk.

"What's this about?" Ryan asked.

Nick and Spencer sat down. Nick studied him evenly. He looked older than he was, with stubble that needed to be shaved. His dirty brown hair stuck up everywhere, like he'd gotten a buzz cut but it had grown out. He was dressed in a long sleeved shirt and jeans that were stained with paint. Did he do something else in addition to bartending?

They started with the basics; his name, age, address. Everything they would need to ensure that they could find him again if they had to.

"Do you know a Julia Rasmath?" Spencer took out a photo of her from the case file, one that Emma had provided. It was Julia in life, not Julia in death.

Ryan's face paled when he saw the photo. Oh, yes,

he did recognize her. "Yeah," he said, but his voice was reluctant.

"How do you know her?" Nick's voice was conversational, and that was how she liked it. It was a conversation, after all. No one was being accused of anything.

Yet.

"I dated her for a while, about a year ago," Ryan answered. His hands shifted in his lap, something Nick noticed and kept an eye on. She didn't want to end up having to defend herself in the interrogation room. That got old, fast.

"How was your relationship?" Spencer asked.

Ryan didn't break eye contact. "It was fine."

"We talked to a friend of Julia's and she doesn't really agree," Nick said, shuffling a couple pieces of paper in front of her. They had only scattered notes, but it was enough to look impressive.

There was a glint of contempt in Ryan's eyes. "I did what I had to do."

Cool water trickled down Nick's spine, anger settling in her stomach. She hated people like Ryan. But, sadly, it wasn't the worst thing she had heard from someone she had interviewed. "So how long did you and Julia date?"

Ryan shrugged. "Six months, maybe."

Nick wrote that down. "How did you meet?"

"At a bar." He leaned back in his chair, his eyes glinting.

Nick didn't know if he was a killer, but he wasn't one of her favorite types of people. "What were you doing yesterday?"

Ryan looked at her, and there was a cruel alertness in his face. "I was sleeping at home. I work night shift at The Dive."

"Could anyone verify your whereabouts?" Spencer pulled out a map. "This is The Dive, right?"

Nick knew the map that Spencer was pointing to. The Dive was located less than a half mile from the condo complex where Julia had lived.

"I left work around four am, went home, had dinner. Went to sleep." He faked a yawn. "Woke up around two or three. Ate breakfast."

"Then what did you do?" Nick asked patiently.

"Stayed at home, watching TV."

"And that led to you being found an hour away, fleeing, how?" Spencer's questions were deceptively laid-back. Nick was intense and focused, Spencer laid-back and seemingly slow.

Ryan shrugged. "I was going to visit family. I wasn't fleeing."

Spencer furrowed his eyebrows, putting his chin on a hand. "Who were you going to visit?"

"My aunt and uncle." Ryan met Spencer's eyes, then Nick's. "They live in Longview."

"What are their names?"

Ryan maintained eye contact. "Marlene and Richard Davis."

Nick would follow up with them to confirm his story. "When did you talk to your aunt and uncle to arrange your trip?"

"It was a spontaneous thing," Ryan said casually. "Like Julia and I."

"How did things end with Julia?" Nick asked, and she put an apologetic tone in the question, so he would think her more compassionate than Spencer.

"I dumped her." Ryan let out a laugh. "She was seeing some other dude. I didn't need her."

The possibility of another person was something Nick had been considering since Melanie had mentioned it, but it was hard to tell whether the mysterious man actually existed, or whether Ryan was trying to push the blame off him onto someone else.

"What do you know about him?" Spencer asked. "Since you're innocent, and all."

"Innocent?" Ryan's eyes narrowed. "What's going on?"

Nick and Spencer exchanged glances. "You don't know?"

"I assumed Julia got in trouble or something." He shrugged. "She had problems with drugs, sometimes," he confided.

Nick jotted that down, with a question mark. Could the drug injected have been recreational, and Julia went there herself? They couldn't take Ryan's word for it. There were some things that would need outside verification. No matter what had happened between Ryan and Julia, they needed to cover all options.

"Julia was found murdered," Nick said softly.

Ryan blinked. "What?"

The surprise on his face seemed real, but Nick had seen some good actors before. There was a reason polygraphs weren't admissible in court.

"She was murdered some time between last night and this morning." They didn't have confirmation of time of death, yet. It had been a cold night and that had slowed decomposition.

"I was working—"

"Until four am, yes." Nick double checked her notes. "What can you tell us about the other man?"

"Not much," Ryan said.

Nick watched as he laced his hands together as he shifted in the chair. Anxiety. He was anxious about something, beyond the circumstances he had already been caught in. What was it?

Everyone had their secrets. It was part of Nick's job to ferret them out.

"I think he was married," Ryan added suddenly. "She was really secretive about him."

Well, if that was true, it added another potential suspect to the mix. But if no one knew who he was, how could they find him? She made a note to grab

Julia's phone records. Maybe she could find a clue there. But with all the technology present these days, it wasn't a guarantee. There were burner phones, Skype, online messaging profiles - there were a million and one ways to communicate, and not all of them were traceable by modern law enforcement.

"Do you know if she had any type of social media?" Spencer asked.

Of the two of them, he was the one that was more tech focused. Nick didn't like spending any extra time on the computer outside of work. She preferred more outside things, like hiking, or hanging out with Lady Grey.

"I don't think so." Ryan looked at her, his eyes dark. "She was pretty private." He brushed some light colored hair off his shirt, his attention turning away from the detectives. "Anything else?" His voice was cool.

"I wouldn't plan to leave town any time soon." Spencer met his gaze.

Inwardly, Nick smiled. "If you want to visit with your aunt and uncle, they'll have to come visit you."

Ryan inclined his head.

"Is there anyone that can confirm your alibi?" Nick asked again.

Ryan considered the question more seriously this time. "Jade might have seen me leave." He shifted his gaze towards Nick. "I went home alone, for once."

Nick narrowly avoided rolling her eyes. Really, this wasn't a dick measuring contest. "Can you give us Jade's name and number?" Spencer gave him something to write with.

Ryan looked at the notepad Spencer passed his way, as if considering what he could get away with, but then he wrote a name and number down. "She's a regular at the bar, sometimes works there."

Spencer nodded.

"Can I go now?" Ryan looked between the two of them.

Nick glanced at Spencer, then nodded once. "Stay nearby."

Ryan didn't say anything, instead he stood and headed towards the door.

"I'll show you out." Spencer opened the door, not waiting for Ryan to follow behind him as he made his way down the hallways towards the entrance.

Nick sat there, jotting down as much of what had happened as she could remember. It was true they had the recording, but she preferred to get impressions written down when they were fresh in her mind. Ryan could be their killer - but there could be someone else.

Maybe this wouldn't be one of those forty-eight hour homicides, after all.

CHAPTER EIGHT

Wednesday, September 14th, 2016. 7:57pm.

Emma sat in her car, tapping her thumbs on the steering wheel. She had just finished talking to Rachel and finalizing Gemma's transfer back to Belle's House. After the recent incident, she was spending more time than ever back at the condos. The other therapists had taken over her House duties, allowing her to focus on the investigation.

She hadn't heard back from Nick after the interviews. Not that it was entirely surprising. Surely Nick had other things to be doing... but it still rankled.

Emma glanced over to the tape still protecting both the crime scene and Julia's home, tempted. Maybe she could go take a peek. She'd be wearing gloves, after all. It'd preserve the evidence. Right?

What she was doing was wrong, and she knew it.

But she had to find out what had happened. She had to figure out what had happened to Julia, and ensure that it didn't happen to anyone else. She put on her leather gloves, so she wouldn't leave any fingerprints.

She opened the door to the empty condo. It was unlocked, the door creaking in the twilight of the evening sun. It was mostly set, the faint rays sending a golden glow over the neighborhood. She closed the door behind her, and the condo was cast into darkness. She grabbed the flashlight she had hooked to her belt loop and turned it on.

The bright beam hit the floor, illuminating the dust and the dried blood that still covered the floor and walls. Apparently, the crime scene cleaners hadn't been by yet.

It was haunting, seeing what she knew was Julia's blood. Where Julia's body had laid. It was the first time she had been at the actual scene, and her stomach churned, bile rising in her throat. She tried to force the images out of her head, but she knew they would stick around.

The fake hardwood floor squeaked underneath her feet as she moved forward. She could see the kitchen from where she was, oddly sterile-looking. The oven was there and cold, the fridge humming softly. She could see the cupboards, a few doors left open as if they had been searched or left unfinished.

She headed into the kitchen. She couldn't stand to

start in the living room, where Julia's body had been. There wasn't any blood in the kitchen.

Starting on the right side, she opened the cupboards. The first few were empty. Then the fridge. There was food in it, though. Not much - a package of bread. Some jam and old apples. Had they been there when the police had searched?

The cupboard had some peanut butter and some saltines. Was someone living there? How had that food gotten in there? Nick hadn't mentioned it. Emma made a mental note to ask. Politely. Each food stuff went into a gallon bag, marked with the sharpie where she found it. She was going to take it to Nick.

Done with the kitchen, she took a deep breath. There were two bedrooms to investigate, to see what she could find out. She could see things differently than the police, since she knew Julia. It wasn't the smartest decision, and she knew it, but she was going to do anything she could to help find Julia's killer.

There were three doors down the hallway. One to each side, then the bathroom at the far end. She started with the bedroom to the right. It was mostly empty, except for a large dresser settled against the far wall. The floor creaked badly as Emma walked, and it made her nervous.

Would someone hear her? Would someone call the police? That would be a hilarious conversation. Probably not something she wanted, but she would deal with that if it happened.

She opened the bottom drawers first. There were a few mothballs - how old was the dresser? - but nothing else. Then the second row of drawers, then the third. She stopped on the far right top drawer. She could see something inside, something crumpled up and tucked into the back. Carefully, aware of her gloves, she pulled it out.

The item was a pair of bloodstained jeans with large holes in them.

Her heart racing, she sat them back down in the drawer and pulled out the gallon Ziploc bags that she had tucked in her back pocket. She'd watched TV, she knew how to preserve evidence. Or at least do a rudimentary job of it. The jeans barely fit in the bag, but hey. It worked.

Surely the police hadn't missed this? Nick was too smart to have missed this. The doubt grabbed at her, but she pushed it down. It didn't hurt to double check.

The bathroom and the other bedroom were eerily empty. The dust had been disturbed, and she could see footprints on the floor from where the crime scene techs had been.

She grabbed the Ziploc bags with the evidence she had found and turned off the flashlight. It was starting to get darker now, and she was already at risk of drawing suspicion by being dressed in dark clothes. Still, she wanted a look at Julia's condo, too.

Dropping the bags off in her trunk, she pulled off her sweatshirt and shivered in the cold. It wasn't that bad, but enough that the cold nipped at her bare arms. She changed gloves. Even though her fingerprints were already in Julia's home, she didn't want to contaminate the crime scene even further. Considerate of her, right?

She brought her flashlight, aware that turning on the lights could alert neighbors that there was someone in the condo. But would that really be a bad thing? Using the master key, she opened the front door and walked in. Goosebumps prickled on her neck. The condo looked like it was waiting for Julia to walk in, to come home to the keys and wallet waiting for her.

But she was never going to.

The kitchen had dishes in the sink, and all the cupboards were closed. Emma checked all of the kitchen drawers, just in case Julia had thrown something in one that was important.

But neither the kitchen nor the living room yielded anything that told her more than she already knew.

She headed back to the bedrooms. One was for Julia, the other set up for a roommate who hadn't yet arrived. Julia's room was on the left. Taking a deep breath, Emma pushed open the door. She had been to the condo before, but almost never in the bedroom.

Julia had picked out a floral bedspread, and the room was decorated sparsely but with class.

She started with the nightstand drawer, opening each one in turn. It felt like a violation of her privacy - but Julia was dead. It couldn't get much worse than that.

Neither drawer had anything interesting in them. A notebook that was empty, some knick-knacks. Julia didn't have a lot.

She tapped on one of the drawers, curious. There was something odd about the color of the wood, almost like a gradient.

Using her fingernails, she tapped around the edges, trying to lift up the panel of wood. But it wouldn't budge.

Emma chuckled as quietly as she could. She'd been watching too many crime shows.

She moved to the bed, lifting up the mattress and feeling underneath it. There was nothing on the frame, so she felt underneath of the mattress.

Then she felt it. There was a notebook, or something similar, hidden in the mattress pad. Her heart started racing, and she quickly felt around the edges of the mattress. The mattress pad had to have a zipper somewhere, right? Otherwise Julia wouldn't have been able to get it in there.

If it even was Julia's. Was it the killer's?

Her cheeks flushed, part out of nerves and part out

of laughing at herself. How, exactly, would the killer have hid something in Julia's mattress pad?

"Aha!" She kept her voice low but couldn't help the exclamation of triumph. She found the zipper, carefully unzipping it until she could reach in with a gloved hand and get whatever the object was.

Her eyes widened once she caught sight of it. It was a planner, some type of date book. It had '2016' on the front. So it was this year's.

Why was it tucked into her mattress pad? Part of Emma wasn't surprised. She didn't know all of Julia's background, but quite a few of the women who ended up in her shelter had a background of abuse. It led to a lot of different quirks.

Emma would know, after all.

The gloves were obnoxious, but the last thing she wanted to do was compromise something that could lead to Julia's killer. She flipped the planner open, page by page. It was one of the ones that had a page for every day, where Julia could list tasks, appointments, and anything else she wanted to note for the day. There was a small notes box, too.

Emma was touched to see that the notes box held stickers. Some were smiling, some were sad, some looked angry. Was she tracking her feelings that way? It was something that she had recommended to some of the ladies who were struggling with anxiety or depression - tracking the ratio of good days to bad days allowed them to keep track of when they were doing well and notice struggling before it began.

She paged through the planner until she was at the week before Julia's murder.

Emma had to swallow down the lump that threatened to rise in her throat, the tears that threatened to fall from her eyes. It was still a fresh wound, jagged, the edges bleeding. Logically over time, Emma knew that the feelings would fade. But there was a difference between logic and actual feelings.

There wasn't anything out of the ordinary until Emma got to the day of Julia's murder. There was an extra appointment. It just said 6pm. No notice of who it was, where it was, or any information that could have led to who she was meeting.

Still, it was a clue. A piece of information. Was she meeting the person who had killed her? Or was she meeting someone else?

She tucked the planner into one of the bags. She was going to have to go to the police station and bring what she found. Her heart skipped a beat at the thought of it - and not just thinking about seeing Nick.

What she had done was reckless, and she knew it.

But if it got her one step closer to finding out who killed Julia, she didn't give a damn.

She headed out towards the living room, her gaze lingering on all of the knick-knacks and other belongings Julia had accumulated in her three months living there. She dreaded the job of taking everything down, preparing it for a new resident. Normally they took their belongings with them.

A knock on the door startled Emma. Her heart raced into overtime, fight-or-flight. Did she stay? Did she run? Who was it?

NICK PARKED HER PATROL CAR, the lights off, and then shifted the car into park. The moment she had heard the 911 call, she knew what had been going on.

"We have reports of an intruder near the Rasmuth crime scene." The electronic voice crackled over the radio. "Curly hair, female. Approximately five foot five."

Nick sighed. "I'll take it."

She highly doubted it was a coincidence that the description matched Emma. Not that she, of course, had been paying a ton of attention to Emma, in order to know what she looked like.

Well. Okay, she kind of had. But it wasn't entirely appropriate given the circumstances.

She grabbed her phone, still sitting in the car, and dialed Emma's number. It rang, and rang. No answer.

"For Christ's sake," Nick muttered under her breath. She spotted Emma's car, the change in angle of the crime scene tape. Was she there, or had she made it to Julia's?

Getting out of the car, she stood there for a second, looking around. She didn't want to make a lot of noise, or risk Emma fleeing before she could talk to her. And there was, after all, the slightest chance that it wasn't actually Emma there.

Although in that case, Nick had bigger fish to fry.

She headed up to Julia's door, her footfall as silent as she could make it. There. She could hear a faint rustling. It was either animals that had gotten into Julia's already, or someone moving around in there.

Nick's left hand went to her gun. Her right hand knocked on the door. Better safe than sorry.

"Emma?" Nick said, her voice low but hopefully loud enough to carry inside. "I know you're in there."

There was a pause, and it was quiet enough that Nick could hear the thudding of her heart. What if she was wrong? What if it wasn't Emma, or was perhaps the killer? She'd be in a lot of trouble.

Then the door slowly swung open, revealing Emma standing there. "How'd you know I was here?" Emma asked, her voice disgruntled.

"People tend to notice when there's someone sneaking around in black after a murder," Nick said dryly. "Next time, dress normally."

Emma glanced down at her clothes, her brows furrowed in thought. Then she looked back at Nick. "What do you mean, next time?"

Oh shit. "I'm not exactly condoning this behavior,"

Nick said. But she couldn't blame her for it, either. Nick remembered the day Sarah had died with crystal clarity, as much as she didn't want to. Would she have moved hell and earth to find Sarah's killer? Yes.

"I have to find out who killed her." There was no apology in Emma's voice. "I have to."

Nick let a faint smile curve her lips up. "I know."

"I found some evidence," Emma said.

Nick looked at her, then caught sight of Emma's gloves. Overkill, perhaps, but at least Emma cared. "What did you find?" It pretty much went against any protocol she had ever heard of, but when it came to catching a killer, Nick was willing to bend the rules.

Emma led her to her car, then popped the trunk. "I wore gloves," she explained, "and bagged anything I found in Ziploc bags."

Not perfect, but it worked. "Where, exactly, did you search?"

Emma met her eyes, steady. "Both the crime scene and Julia's home."

"I'm sorry you had to see that," Nick said. And she was. No one should have to see where someone they cared about was murdered.

Was there something more between Emma and Julia? Or was it simply the protectiveness of Emma looking after someone in her charge?

Shoving that out of her mind, she looked at the Ziploc bags that Emma handed her.

"I found some food in the pantry and the fridge," Emma said. "And a pair of bloodstained jeans in a drawer."

Nick narrowed her eyes at the objects, thinking. They hadn't found anything like that in their initial search. Did the crime scene techs miss these items, or had they simply not been there? There had been a rash of break-ins in the area, mostly by homeless people. But what were the odds that someone would pick the scene of a recent murder to break into?

"I'll take them to the station and get them processed," Nick said.

"I found this in Julia's mattress pad." Emma pulled out the Ziploc bag with the journal in it.

Nick itched to touch it. Instead, she just looked at it.

"Here." Emma handed her some thin plastic gloves.

Nick just looked at her, amusement in her eyes. Then she slid the gloves on as Emma slid it out of the Ziploc.

"Look at this." Emma flipped the pages, the planner carefully held in her gloved hand as she turned it to the day of the murder. "There's a meeting she was supposed to have the day she was murdered. 6pm."

"It doesn't say anything about who it's with?" Nick asked, flipping a few pages before and after. Still, excitement made the hairs on the back of her neck stand up. This could be big. This could help them track

Julia's movements and figure out who she had come into contact with right before she died.

Maybe Melanie knew something about the meeting. She had talked to Julia after it, per her testimony.

"No, nothing about who it's with," Emma said ruefully. "And there's nothing in the contacts or anywhere else, either."

Nick stood silent, her eyes on the planner but her mind elsewhere. "You're not going to give up, are you?" She lifted her head to look at Emma.

Emma met Nick's questioning eyes with steely determination. "No."

Part of Nick wanted to smile. She may not like the way Emma went about things, but she had to respect her determination. "In that case, you might as well come over to my place. I have a copy of the case files." Nick paused. "And better coffee than the police station."

CHAPTER NINE

Wednesday, September 14th, 2016. 9:32pm.

A knock on her car window startled Emma, and she stifled a scream. She narrowed her eyes at Nick, who was standing there with an annoying grin on her face. Then Emma rolled down the window.

"Comfortable following me home?" Nick jerked a thumb towards a small blue four-door that was parked not too far away. She had gone into the station to sign the Ziploc bags into evidence, leaving Emma sitting in her car outside the station.

Emma nodded, energy sizzling through her veins. She hadn't gotten nearly enough sleep, and was going to be tired, but Nick had promised her coffee and case files. It was almost like a date.

Not that she would go on a date with Nick. Nope. Not at the moment, anyway.

Once Julia's killer was caught? Well, that was a different story.

Without answering, Nick headed back to her car. Emma watched as she pulled her blazer off, tossing it onto the passenger seat before starting her car.

Emma followed Nick on the short drive home. Nick didn't live too far from her, surprisingly, or from the station. It wasn't something Emma had ever thought of. Not that she spent a lot of time at home.

Nick pulled into the driveway, next to another car. Emma paused, before pulling up to the curb. Was there someone else there? Did Nick have a partner, or someone else?

Nick got out, heading straight to the car next to her.

Emma stayed in her car, uncertain.

Then the door of the stopped car opened and a beautiful woman stepped out.

Emma's heart dropped. She was short-haired like Nick but her hair was slightly longer, and she had warm brown eyes and a radiant smile.

Nick hugged her, then peered into the car. Emma could see the vague outline of a second person.

Okay, Emma had been promised case files and coffee. People hadn't been included! There was also the flicker of jealousy. She wasn't jealous. Even if she liked Nick – and okay, she sort of did, a little bit – relationships weren't worth it. No matter how nice someone seemed on the surface, it wasn't worth the risk.

Nope.

Emma opened her door, slowly getting out of the car. She could hear Nick's voice.

Then a dog jumped out of the car, and Nick's attention turned to the dog. It was a small-medium dog, maybe twenty five or thirty pounds, and it was trying to jump into Nick's arms, baying as it did so. Tricolor, with a black saddle, brown smudges, and white paws and tip of the tail.

Nick smiled down at the dog, then leaned down and picked her up, allowing the dog - a beagle? - to lick her face. "Hi girl," Nick said, her voice warm. She turned to the two people in the car. "Thank you for watching her."

Oh. They were watching the dog?

"You coming, Emma?" Nick looked down at her, the beagle still struggling in her arms. Nick's face was slightly scrunched as she tried to evade the long tongue of the very happy dog.

"Yup." Emma grabbed her purse, heading up onto the driveway, trying to conceal a smile. The lights of the first car were on, now, although the driver hadn't yet gotten back in her seat.

"This is Jordan, and her fiancée Carys." Nick nodded to the driver, then the woman in the car. "They watch Lady Grey for me when I have to work."

Oh. Not that Emma was happy neither of them were dating Nick. Nope. "Nice to meet you." She shook

Jordan's hand, and exchanged polite nods with the redhead in the car.

"You owe us now." Jordan winked.

Nick mock-saluted her. "Have a good night."

Emma followed Nick out of the way as Jordan got into the car and then backed out of the driveway.

"I watch their dog and horse sometimes, and in return they watch Lady Grey," Nick explained.

"Ah," Emma said with a nod. She turned to look at the dog in Nick's arms. "This is Lady Grey?"

"Yup." Nick stroked the brown head.

Lady Grey was looking quizzically at Emma, her black nose twitching as she took her in.

"Can I pet her?" They had things to do, and Emma knew it, but c'mon - who could resist a dog?

"Of course." Nick shifted so that she had a better hold on the dog. "She likes to wiggle."

Emma grinned, then came closer, reaching out and scratching Lady Grey behind her ear. "She's sweet." Lady Grey licked her hand.

"Ready to go inside?" Nick looked at her, eyes warm.

Emma nodded, then followed her to the door. Instead of a key, Nick had a keypad. She typed in a code, and Emma heard the door unlock.

"Fancy," Emma whistled.

Nick's smile was grim. "I take safety very seriously."

"You're not from here, are you?"

"Kind of." Nick pushed the door open, allowing Emma in before she shut it. Then she put Lady Grey down, who immediately went over and started sniffing Emma's legs. Nick wandered into the kitchen, Emma following her.

"What do you mean?" Emma kept the question casual. She was curious, but if it was something sensitive, Nick wasn't obligated to open up to her.

Nick was quiet, her attention on what was obviously a routine well established. She pulled down a dog bowl, filled it with two scoops of food, and grabbed something from the fridge and squirted a tablespoon of it onto the food before mixing it in with a plastic spoon.

"Lady Grey is both picky and spoiled," Nick said, her attention now on mixing the food.

Emma smiled. That she could understand. Her gaze shifted through the kitchen, and lingered on a few of the photos. They were of Nick and another woman. She had blonde hair, cut in a short bob, and was obviously happy. A friend?

Then she saw the matching rings on their hands. No, not a friend. A partner. A wife? It was legal now.

"I grew up not far from here," Nick said, her attention on Lady Grey as she sat the food bowl down. "Went to college in California. Met Sarah there."

When Emma looked back at Nick, she saw Nick was watching her with a sad smile on her face.

"She died in the line of duty," Nick said, and her voice was as sad as her expression. "She's been gone three and a half years now."

"I'm sorry," Emma said, and she was. What else was there to say to that? "I've never found a woman I loved enough to marry."

Nick's eyebrows raised a hair. Emma smiled ruefully. So they were both gay, then. Or at least both interested in women.

"Ready to look at the case files?" Nick changed the topic, something Emma was grateful for.

Emma nodded, then cast one last look at the photos on the wall before she followed Nick towards the living room.

She stopped, her eyes wide. It was like in a movie. There was a combined whiteboard/cork board against the far wall, files and papers dotting the coffee table, couch, a few on the floor. "The case isn't even forty eight hours old," Emma said, a bit dazed.

Nick shrugged. "These aren't all for Julia's case," she said, working on clearing a spot for Emma. The jingling sound of Lady Grey's collar announced her return. "But I like to be prepared."

Emma understood that. "What am I allowed to look at?"

Nick hesitated for a split second, then settled on the floor. One hand was scratching Lady Grey behind the ears, the other one sorting out various piles. "This is the autopsy report," she said, tucking it underneath a few other things. "And photos of the crime scenes." Her voice was quiet. "You probably don't want to look at those."

Emma felt cold rush over her. "No, thanks." Not unless she had to.

"Here's a list of the evidence we found and the various photos we took of Julia's home and the rest of the crime scene." Nick pushed them towards her. "We took statements from many of the people living nearby, and those are included in this file."

Emma picked them up. "Do you have a copy of the appointment book?"

Nick stared at her. "The department isn't that fast."

"I think that six pm appointment is something we should follow up on," Emma said.

"And we will, when we get the copy." Nick grinned, and the lightness in her expression made Emma's chest tighten.

She had to change the topic. "Where should I start?"

That caught Nick off guard, and she blinked at Emma before a smile tugged at the corner of her lips. "Start with the statements. You know quite a few of the people involved, see if they match up with what you know."

Emma took the files, and started reading.

The first was Rachel's statement. The scream. No

dog barking. Then there was her neighbor's, then another.

"Did they ever figure out time of death?" Emma lifted her head to look at Nick. Lady Grey was curled into a ball near their feet.

"Somewhere between ten pm and three am," Nick said absently. "With some wiggle room."

"So it's not like it is on TV?" Emma half-smiled.

Nick chuckled. "I wish."

"Do you have something to write with?" Emma asked.

Nick passed her a notepad with pens. "You can use the whiteboard, too."

Emma sat the notepad down for a second and then walked over to the whiteboard that covered most of the far wall. How did she get the whiteboard to stay on the wall, especially at that size?

"Left side is for this case."

Emma nodded, turning to the left side. She picked up the marker, writing Julia's name in the middle. Then she circled it, like a mind map she had done in school a long time ago.

"What do you know so far?" Emma asked, turning to look at Nick.

"We traced a prior boyfriend named Ryan to a bar, where he works," Nick said, looking up from the folder.

Emma wrote "Ryan" and then circled it, drawing a

line from Julia's bubble to Ryan's and writing 'ex' over it.

"Did Julia talk about him in therapy? I've started going through the notes, but I haven't finished." Nick sat the file Emma had sent her on the table.

"Can I see it?" Lady Grey lifted her head at Emma's voice, then laid it back down with a dramatic sigh.

Nick pushed it towards her.

Emma picked it up, flicking through her notes. Julia had been in Belle's House for quite some time, and Julia had continued her therapy once she was at the halfway house.

She flipped all the way back to the beginning, the intake notes from the very first session.

"Let's talk about what brought you here today." It was the question Emma hated asking, but it was one of the most important ones.

Julia looked at the ground. Her eyes were hollow, and one was black. There were scrapes on her knuckles, and bruises dotting her arms. There were probably more Emma couldn't see. "I fell in love with the wrong man."

Emma nodded, but didn't write anything down. She had her legs crossed, one over the other, and the notepad was on her lap.

"Can you tell me how you left?" Emma asked. It wasn't unusual to have to drag details out. Emma wouldn't pry much this first session, just enough to be able to fill out the paperwork. The rest could come in time.

"He hit me with a beer bottle," she said softly. "He threw me against the wall. And I realized he was going to kill me." There was a bitter twist to her lips. *"He may still kill me."*

"Can you tell me about him?" Emma jotted down a few notes. Fear of the perpetrator. Many of their women were afraid, and Emma couldn't blame them.

Julia shook her head.

Emma sat in silence, waiting. Sometimes waiting was the best strategy.

"He has friends in high places," Julia said finally. "I could die, and nothing would happen to him."

"That's not true," Emma said, but even she didn't fully believe that. While the justice system tried its best, it wasn't perfect.

"You said Ryan works at a bar?" Emma frowned at the notes. A bartender could have friends in high places, but it wasn't as likely.

"Yes." Nick grabbed another folder, then her phone. "We talked to him, he claimed to be at the bar until four am. His coworker confirmed that was his shift end, but he was allowed a half-hour break that he took some time between 1 and 3, and they can't account for where he was."

"So that's enough time?" Emma considered, and then wrote '1-3' next to his bubble.

"The Dive, where he works, is less than half a mile from the condo complex." Nick flicked through her phone. "Spencer timed it – that's my partner – and it's possible."

Emma nodded. Then she wrote 6pm, circled it, and drew a line with a question mark.

"Was there anything else in the appointment book that you thought was unusual?" Nick sat cross-legged, Lady Grey next to her.

Emma thought back, trying to picture the planner in her mind. Then she shook her head. "There was work, a few social things. Nothing that jumped out at me besides that."

Nick nodded, flipping through some photos. Emma caught sight of them out of the corner of her eyes. She could see the blood, the close-ups of Julia's body.

Inwardly she shuddered. She didn't want to see those images.

Emma sat there, her gaze on the case files, but her mind quite a ways away. She put the whiteboard marker down, picked up the file full of statements and sat next to Nick on the couch. She was taller than Nick this way, since Nick was on the floor next to her. But she liked being close to her, Lady Grey between the two of them.

"What if there was a second person?" Nick looked up at her.

"What did Ryan say about their relationship?" Emma flicked through the statements. She could read his, but she wanted to hear it from Nick.

Nick related what had happened in the interview, what he'd said.

Distaste flashed across Emma's face. She hated the people who hurt others in the name of love. It was why she wanted to avoid love in the first place.

It didn't matter that Nick had warm dark blue eyes, or that the way she smiled sent goosebumps prickling down Emma's arms. Nor the fact that Nick's attentive, focused expression was attractive as she looked at Emma. Nick cared about Julia, even if she didn't know her.

Nick's phone rang. Emma flinched, then laughed at herself. Holding up a finger, Nick took the call. Her face was troubled when she hung it up. "They sent the jeans to the lab to process for DNA evidence."

"How long will that take?" It was easy to feel apprehensive with the expression on Nick's face.

"Hopefully a week."

"Hopefully?"

"A week." Nick's face was stubborn.

Emma studied her for a moment, then smiled. Nick was going to do her best, just like Emma was.

"Ryan could have been the person who sent her to Belle's House," Emma said thoughtfully. "I'd look into his family, see if he has any connections higher up."

Nick jotted that down. "What did you think of Rachel's statement?" Her voice was carefully neutral.

"What do you mean?" Emma narrowed her eyes.

"She's the only one that reported a scream in the entire complex," Nick said.

Emma considered that. "Maybe she was the only one close enough to hear it."

"Or maybe she was lying," Nick countered.

Emma scowled, but it was a possibility. She tried not to think her ladies would do such things, but they were human, after all. "Why would she lie?"

"Maybe she was doing something that she shouldn't have been?" Nick shrugged. "What are the rules?"

"Check in once a day, therapy weekly. Visit Belle's House for twice-monthly group therapy. Meet with their case manager, work towards becoming an independent and getting their own house." Emma ticked them off on her fingers. She was quiet for a few seconds, thinking.

"Was she seeing someone?" Nick asked.

Emma shook her head. "That's another thing; no relationships when in the house. They are allowed outside friendships."

"Maybe she was meeting a friend."

"But why didn't she put in the name?" Emma countered.

"Maybe it was a romantic friend," Nick suggested.

"Maybe." Emma was somewhat doubtful. "We need to look into it more."

"And we will," Nick agreed.

Emma smiled at her, and silence hung between

them. She hesitated, then reached and put her hand on Nick's shoulder.

Nick looked up at her.

"Thank you," Emma said, and she meant it with all of her heart.

Nick studied her, then reached up and put a hand on hers, a smile on her lips. It sent warmth surging through Emma's body. "Any time."

CHAPTER TEN

Wednesday, September 14th, 2016. 8:22pm.

"I hope this isn't a serial killer." He looked at the man in front of him, laughed a fake laugh. Waved goodbye and left the building. What did they know? The detective hadn't said much. He would have to look at the files they had.

Did they know his name? Where he worked? Had Julia ever mentioned him? He doubted it. She was smarter than that, even if she had left him.

Then the idea struck him. Serial killer. What if he made it look like a serial killer, something completely random? That could destroy any personal links to a killer, if they ever figured out who he was. He sat in his car, tapping his fingers roughly on the steering wheel. Yes, that would work. Wouldn't it?

He drove in silence for a while. He was almost home, where his wife and son were waiting. His family.

Yes. Yes, that would do.

He nodded to himself as he got out of his car, heading towards the shed that was on the far side of the house. His wife's gardening supplies were kept there, as was his son's sports stuff. He pushed open the door, searching the dim space. He hadn't meant to hit Julia with the fireplace poker. He just remembered grabbing it, then slamming it into her head, again and again.

He had to replicate something like that.

Then his eyes fell on his son's baseball bat. That would work. It was convenient. Anthony had given up baseball practice. He wouldn't need it.

He tucked the baseball bat under his arm. Getting back in his car, he drove back towards the complex where everything had started. He wanted to make it random, but connected. Maybe someone was targeting that complex, not a single woman.

That would cast doubt on him being the killer if they ever found out who he was. Besides, they would be too busy chasing their own tails. He had made sure of it.

He knew exactly who his next target would be. She wasn't as bad as Julia, no, but she had still wronged him. The world would be better off without her.

After all, he did good work. He didn't deserve to get caught. Other people did, though. The bad people. He was responsible for locking bad people away.

Too bad someone had to die to keep it that way.

CHAPTER ELEVEN

Thursday, September 15th, 2016. 9:45am.

Emma took a deep breath, her hands on the steering wheel. She had slept over at Nick's (on the couch), and now it was time to check in on Rachel and Tansy. It was time to do her rounds of the few women still in the halfway houses. Rachel was up first.

To get to Rachel's condo, she had to go near Julia's. Sitting in her car, Emma could lift her head to the right and see the building. The crime scene tape was gone, and the condo had been cleaned. Once her murder was solved, they would move someone new in.

Hopefully it would be soon, but Emma knew that wasn't likely. The domestic violence shelters in the cities were overflowing. She hated turning away women, and would do everything she could to avoid having to do so.

She didn't regret breaking into Julia's condo. If it helped the police solve the murder, if it helped them bring justice to whomever did it, she'd do it over and over again.

She finally turned the car off, grabbing her purse and stepping out of the car. It was morning now, the sun shining dimly in the sky behind the fluffy clouds. She liked Washington for that reason. Rarely hot and, even if the sun was out, it was often hidden behind the clouds.

Emma closed the door of her car and leaned against it. Her notepad and pen were in her purse, along with everything else she needed. It was just a follow-up assessment, in the wake of Julia's murder. It wasn't anything super serious. Yet Emma couldn't help the anxiety that rushed through her.

"It makes sense," Emma murmured to herself. After what had happened with Julia, it was only natural to feel anxious about returning to the complex. Right?

She headed up the walkway. Rachel's car was in the driveway, the light was on in the living room. A relieved smile came to Emma's face. She worried way too much.

It would be fine.

She knocked on the door, waited.

No answer.

Anxiety fluttered in her stomach but she tried to

quell it. Maybe Rachel was just sleeping, maybe she didn't hear the knock.

Emma knocked louder, hard enough that her knuckles ached. Rachel had to be sleeping.

Still no answer.

Throwing caution to the wind, she tried the doorknob. It was locked.

No. No. It had to be something else.

She hit her elbow against the door, hearing the lock give. She didn't normally break down her own doors, but this was a special circumstance. She had to know. Surely Rachel was sleeping inside.

The door gave with a loud sound, splintering. Emma stopped.

Rachel was on the floor, her eyes staring at nothing. Her head was covered in red, her black hair stained with coagulated blood. Blood spatter decorated the ceiling, the walls. There was a smeared path on the floor, as if she had been moved.

Emma's breath came faster, adrenaline making her head spin. "No, no," she cried, but she didn't hear her own words. Was she even speaking out loud?

She fell to her knees, screamed. "No!"

Oh god, no.

"Emma?"

She didn't know how long passed before she heard Nick's voice. She was staring at nothing, could barely feel the warmth of Nick's hand on her shoulder.

Nick helped her to her feet, but Emma couldn't see her. The world was fuzzy around her. She heard people talking, but their words didn't make sense.

Then someone put their arm around her, led her out of the house, to the side. There were fewer people. Emma could feel the springiness of the grass underneath her feet, the slight give of no concrete.

"Breathe in," Nick's quiet voice said in her ear. "Hold it for five seconds, then breathe out."

Emma closed her eyes, her hands latching onto Nick's shoulder, holding onto her as if she was the only thing keeping her up. And she was, in a way. But she breathed in, held it. Counted to five in her head, and then let it out.

She could hear more voices now, hear the soft chatter of people talking. The image of Rachel's body, the eyes staring, was burned into her mind.

Emma clenched her eyes shut. Breathed. She wasn't going to let it break her. She was stronger than that. She could help Nick get justice for both women.

Her lips trembled, and she focused on stilling them.

"Emma?" Nick kept her hand on Emma's shoulder.

Emma reached up and put her hand on Nick's, drawing comfort from her closeness.

Nick wrapped her arms around Emma, drawing her close.

Emma hesitated, but then let herself be held. She could tuck her head in the crook between Nick's neck and shoulder, breathe in. She smelled woodsy, with an evergreen undertone. She wasn't going to cry, but the image of Rachel's body was burned in her mind.

She took another deep breath, then lifted her head. She didn't let go of Nick, and Nick didn't let go of her. "Sorry."

"You're in shock," Nick said, leaning in and pressing her cheek to Emma's. It felt oddly intimate, but Emma liked it. It didn't mean anything, right? It was just some innocent comfort. "Let's get you a blanket." She pressed her lips very briefly to Emma's forehead, then let go of her. Then she stopped for a moment, as if realizing what she'd done.

Their eyes met. Part of Emma wanted to run away. She wasn't ready for that, didn't want it. But part of her wanted Nick to do it again. To kiss her again and again, until she couldn't think of anything else.

Emma tried to smile, and reached out and squeezed Nick's hand in understanding. She wasn't sure what it was, but they could figure that out later when they weren't at a crime scene.

Without saying anything, Nick led her towards the ambulance that had arrived, grabbing a blanket and swirling it around Emma's shoulders.

It was oddly warm for such a light blanket, and it felt like Emma was being wrapped in a hug. Then she lifted her head slightly, felt Nick's arms around her again, holding her close. "I'm sorry." Nick pressed her cheek back against Emma's. Emma could feel her weight shift under her as Nick settled against the ambulance, allowing Emma to brace herself in Nick's arm.

Nick stroked Emma's hair, gentle around the curls. It should have felt silly, infantilizing, but all Emma wanted to do was pull her closer. "I'm so sorry you had to see that."

Tears threatened to swamp Emma but she shoved them back. She was stronger than that. She wasn't going to cry.

"I have to check on my ladies," Emma said, and she sounded like a robot. "I have one more to see."

"What number is she in?" Nick reached down to her belt and grabbed the radio that was there, she then spoke into it.

"Number?" Emma looked at her, the cotton ball of feelings still making her head feel fuzzy.

"What's her address?" Nick clarified.

Another person showed up, standing just to Nick's side.

"This is Allison," Nick said. "I'm going to have her check on the last lady for you."

"But -" Emma tried to protest.

"No buts," Nick said, her voice firm but soft.

Reluctantly Emma gave the name and address. Nick was the police, and Emma trusted her.

"You'll need to give us your statement." Nick's voice was quieter. "And I want to get you out of here."

Emma swallowed almost painfully. She could hear the creaking of wheels as the ME's staff took the gurney out of the home. Hot tears threatened to spill. It was Rachel's body on that gurney, just as it had been Julia's.

What were the news people saying? Would anyone even miss the two women?

"Did you hear anything out about the evidence I found?" Emma felt wooden.

Nick made a questioning noise.

"From the house." Emma paused. "Julia's house."

Nick's hand tightened slightly on Emma's shoulders. "DNA tests came back. A homeless man named Brent Dallas. We went and talked to him, but he's got an alibi."

"What?" Emma looked at Nick, alarmed.

"He was in jail the night Julia died," Nick explained. "He was released the day after. He was probably living in the condo illegally and fled when he heard you coming."

Emma crumpled into Nick's grip. So much for catching Julia's killer that way. Were they even the same killer? Were they chasing two people?

"How did you get here?" Emma asked. It had been lurking at the back of her mind, how Nick had found her.

"A neighbor heard your screaming and called 911," Nick said. There was a rueful smile on her face. "You have quite the lungs."

Emma tried to smile but couldn't.

"Would you be okay coming with me to the station?" Nick exchanged glances with someone over Emma's head.

Emma hesitated, then nodded. "Then I need to go back to Belle's House," she said. "We have a memorial to plan."

Nick hugged her a bit closer, trying to comfort her. "I'll be right back."

Emma tracked her out of the corner of her eyes, watching as she headed over to Spencer. Probably to tell him what she was doing. She turned her gaze to the pavement, her attention drifting. Rachel was dead.

No. She couldn't be dead. She couldn't be gone. But she was.

She was going to have to go back to Belle's House, tell everyone. She pulled the blanket tighter around her, finding comfort in its warmth. But it wasn't as good as Nick's arms.

It wasn't long before Nick was back, standing just in front of her. "Ready to go?"

Emma looked at her, then back at her car.

"I'll drive you," Nick said. "When we're done I can bring you back to your car or drop you off at Belle's House."

"Where's your officer?" Emma's eyes flickered back to Nick. "The one that's going to check on Tansy."

Nick picked up the radio from her waist. She pressed a button. "Is Allison back?"

There was a crackle. "Yes. Tansy's fine, and Allison is taking her to Belle's House now."

Emma almost sagged in relief. Belle's House had good security. Tansy would be safe there, and Emma could prevent this from ever happening again.

Nick guided her to her car, and Emma got inside, buckling herself up out of habit. The ride to the station was blissfully short, and before she knew it she and Nick were sitting in one of the small interrogation rooms. It was dismal, just like it was in the movies.

The walls were a stark grey, the table bolted to the floor. Even the chairs were bolted down. How many people had thrown them before they had decided to do that?

"Sorry," Nick said, and there was a true apology in her voice. "Our nicer rooms are under construction."

Emma shook her head. "It's fine." And it was. It didn't matter, really. Not any more.

"Are you up to talking about what you saw?" Nick asked gently.

Emma lifted her eyes to meet Nick's. "How can you do this every day?"

Nick's face was sad. "Sometimes I don't know. But

it's worth it when we can catch whoever is hurting other people."

Emma let out a slow exhale, then nodded. "What do you need to know?"

Thursday, September 15th, 2016. 2:41pm.

"I GOT THE PHONE RECORDS." Spencer's voice pulled Nick out of her reverie.

"Awesome." Nick reached out a hand for them. Her mind was halfway across the city, thinking about Emma back at Belle's House. She was probably already planning the double memorial.

Spencer was in charge of getting the phone records for both Julia and Rachel. After searching all the public records she could get her hands on, Emma had finally found Rachel's parents. Rachel had been legally estranged from her parents when she was sixteen. She had been on her own. The whereabouts of her parents were unknown.

It broke Nick's heart, seeing so many women without people who loved them. Rachel's parents were somewhere unknown. Julia's were dead. Not that Nick hadn't seen it before. She was a homicide detective, after all. She still didn't like it.

Nick pulled out the phone records, separating

them. "Do we have the ones from Belle's House?"

Spencer shook his head. "Emma's assured us she'll get them to us in the next 48 hours. They keep a log of who uses the House phone."

Nick nodded, her mind churning as she looked over Julia's list. The call logs were a lot sparser than she had expected. Only a few calls a day. Most were to Belle's House, occasionally to phones that belonged to the other ladies.

Rachel's seemed more normal. Tons of texts and phone calls. There were a lot to a single number. Nick highlighted it. It was a local area code, but those weren't very specific. Besides, people could move. It didn't mean that it was someone nearby.

Logic told her that Julia and Rachel's murders were connected, and that there was a decent chance Belle's House was being targeted for a reason. It wasn't likely that a killer would choose two women in the same program by accident. But they had lived close to each other. Maybe it was a coincidence. Maybe he had something against the condo complex.

"Anything else on Julia's phone?" Nick lifted her head, drawing Spencer's attention.

"Nope." Spencer leaned back in his chair. "Something wrong?"

"There's just so little." Nick shuffled the papers. "Not that many texts, not that many phone calls. It's not what you would expect for someone her age."

"Maybe she just doesn't talk a lot," Spencer suggested.

"Maybe," Nick allowed. But she didn't think it was likely. "Maybe she had a burner." They were easy to get nowadays, and easy for people to use. Someone who had been on the run at some point might use one. But if she had one, where had it gone? Had the killer taken it? If so, why?

The phone rang and Spencer picked it up, listening to the other end. "We'll be over in a sec." He hung it up.

"ME?" Nick sat up a bit straighter.

"Yup. They finished Rachel's autopsy. Priority," he added.

"We might have a serial killer?" Nick was already packing her belongings up.

This time it was Nick's phone that was ringing. She stopped, picking it up and tucking it between her shoulder and her ear. "Hello?"

"This is Nancy at the front desk. Someone is here saying that she was Rachel's girlfriend?" Nancy was the department's secretary.

Nick immediately pushed the speaker button and sat the phone down. "Can you say that again?"

"Someone is here claiming to be Rachel's girlfriend," Nancy repeated patiently.

Nick and Spencer exchanged looks. "I'll take this, you go get the report from the ME," Nick said.

Spencer nodded in agreement. "I'll send you the report when I get it."

Nick unpacked her notepad, then picked up the phone again, taking it off speaker. "I'll be right out there, Nancy."

"I'll let her know." The call ended.

Why, exactly, hadn't Nick asked for a name?

It was the little things.

Thankfully one of the smaller rooms was open, where they could talk and it didn't look like she was going to be interrogated. Girlfriend? Did that mean a friend or a romantic partner?

Yay for language ambiguity.

Nick headed out of the back corner, her small notepad firmly tucked in her breast pocket. It was easy to find the woman she was supposed to be talking to. She was standing, her head down. She looked maybe twenty, dressed in coveralls that hung on her thin frame. She wasn't exactly the type of person Nick had been expecting, but she'd long learned to expect the unexpected.

"This is Detective Tanner," Nancy said, her voice loud enough to catch the girl's attention.

The girl - the woman - lifted her head, and met Nick's gaze. She didn't speak. She seemed to be in shock, tears still streaming down her cheeks. Her eyes were red, and pink splotches were on her face and neck. She had been crying for quite some time.

"What's your name?" Nick asked, already able to tell she would have to handle this gently.

"Kylie." Her eyes were distant, but she was paying attention to Nick. "I was Rachel's girlfriend."

Was there a polite way to ask friend vs girlfriend? Even as a lesbian it wasn't something Nick had ever figured out. And this, especially, tugged at her. She had lost Sarah a few years ago, but it still hurt. She knew what poor Kylie was going through.

"Rachel and I had been dating for two months." Kylie sniffed, pulling her phone out of her pocket and staring at it. "I keep expecting her to call."

Well, that answered that question. "Are you okay to come with me so we can talk in private?"

Kylie nodded.

Nick led her through the back part of the department to one of the private rooms they used to talk to families, or for more sensitive discussions. It was the better place for this sort of talk, even with the construction.

"So you and Rachel were dating?" Nick asked. Kylie nodded again.

Although Nick doubted a woman was capable of the killings, Kylie could still provide them with some evidence that they needed. Maybe the cases weren't related.

There was just so much they didn't know.

CHAPTER TWELVE

Thursday, September 15th, 2016. 2:55pm.

"What prompted you to come forward?" Nick asked, her voice gentle. She could guess - it didn't take long before news of the murders were on the TV, even if the identities weren't released. But maybe they were wrong. Maybe Kylie was the killer. After all, they didn't have the autopsy report yet.

Kylie looked down at the table. "I saw the news." She wiped some tears away from her cheeks. "They showed her picture."

Of course they did. Nick had no idea how they'd got it. The media drove her nuts. "Kylie, do you know anything about the night that Rachel was killed?"

Kylie shook her head. "I stayed over on Tuesday. The night that other girl was killed?" She met Nick's eyes with watery green ones.

Nick felt adrenaline surge through her. Could Kylie connect the cases? "Did you hear anything that night?"

Kylie hesitated, then nodded. "My dog started barking around one am," she admitted.

"Did either of you hear a scream?" Nick could picture Rachel's statement.

Kylie shook her head. "Rachel didn't want to admit that I was there. They're not allowed to have relationships when they're still associated with the House."

That made sense. It wasn't the worst secret someone had been hiding.

"If the killer—" Kylie took a shuddery breath. "If Rachel's killer spent any time in her condo, they would have got dog hair on themselves." Her smile was sad. "Quentin, my dog, sheds a lot."

"Do you have—"

"A sample of his hair?" Kylie dug into her purse.

That wasn't exactly what Nick had been about to ask, but it worked. "Yes."

"Here." Kylie pushed the bag across. "The vet pulled them out to make sure the roots were attached."

Nick took the baggie, reaching onto one of the shelves and pulling down an evidence bag. She had no idea if they would ever need the evidence, but it was better to have it than to regret not having it.

"Is there anything else you remember?" Nick asked, keeping her voice gentle.

Kylie nodded again. "Rachel's ex-boyfriend had been leaving nasty messages on her voicemail."

"We didn't find any voicemails on her phone." This piqued Nick's attention.

"Rachel may have deleted them," Kylie said. "She was getting really frustrated with the calls."

Still, it was something they could look into. "What kind of phone calls?"

A shiver went through Kylie's body. *"I hate you, you'll regret leaving me.* That sort of thing." Her lips thinned. "Nasty."

Nick noted this down. She wanted to write it down, cement it in her memory, but she didn't want to distress Kylie more than she had to. "Do you have any way to find the ex-boyfriend?"

"His name is Conner." Kylie's lips twisted in a hint of a frown. "I don't know if he has a job, but he's local."

This time Nick grabbed her notepad and jotted this down. "Do you have a last name?"

"Maddison, maybe?" Kylie shrugged helplessly. "She didn't really talk about him."

Nick nodded, understanding. "Would you mind giving us your number so we can exclude you when we're looking at the phone records?" Exclusion wasn't the right word, but it would allow them to check her honesty and make sure they weren't being fed a tale. But Kylie sounded genuine.

Kylie gave it to her, then wiped a few tears from her face. "Is there anything else?"

Nick shook her head. "If we have any more questions for you I'll get in touch, okay?" Nick's smile was sad. She knew what it was like to lose someone unexpectedly, no matter how long you had been together. Loss was never easy, whether it was after weeks or months.

She walked Kylie out and bade her goodbye. As she watched the small woman disappear out the front doors, she saw Spencer coming in. "Done already?" Nick asked.

"Got the report and everything," Spencer said, waving the folder at her. He headed towards the back where their offices were, an urgency to his pace. "Going to fill me in on the girlfriend?"

Nick did, giving him the short summary.

Spencer sank into his chair. Nick took the folder, opening it and quickly reading the autopsy report summary. Her eyebrows raised. Blunt force trauma in the same part of the head. But what was different was the lack of drug marks. And she had been killed in her own home.

Toxicology was back on Julia. They had found diazepam in her system, a common sedative also known as valium.

"So we're thinking drugs were used to move Julia?" Nick's eyes flickered to Spencer and then back to the report in front of her. Was Julia more or less important? Was it more personal to kill a victim in their home or not?

"Probably," Spencer said. He turned to his computer and started typing. "But you know what I think about coincidences."

Nick smiled wryly. That was true. "We need to look into Rachel's ex-boyfriend," she said. "There's a *chance* the cases aren't connected." She let out a sigh.

Spencer snorted.

"It needs to be ruled out," Nick said with a shrug. It wasn't likely, but everything had to be explored. "I'm going to call Emma." The thought filled Nick with both giddiness and dread. It was worth it, to solve this case. Emma could help her fill in some of the missing pieces. Maybe she hadn't known about Kylie, but since Rachel was another victim, maybe Emma knew more about her, too.

"Let me know if you find anything out," Spencer instructed. Then he turned his full attention to the computer.

Then Nick dialed the number she had already memorized.

"Hello?" Emma's voice was shaky but warm.

It made Nick smile. "I've got some news."

Thursday, September 15th, 2016. 4:12pm.

EMMA CONSIDERED the implications of Nick's call, already digging through the records Belle's House kept of who used the phone when. It wasn't personally supervised, but the ladies were supposed to sign a log.

Not that it always happened.

It was easy to find once she figured out what months they had been there. There was some overlap, too. A couple of months. She didn't have the outgoing calls quite yet, but when they arrived, Nick would be able to find out who had made what calls.

It didn't stop them from getting a burner phone, but those were much harder to get in a DV shelter. Or even out of it.

Security alerted her when Nick arrived. They were going to go out to the storage space, where Emma and the other staffers kept all the belongings of prior residents, both home-based and out in the community.

Heading downstairs from her office, the records in hand, she met Nick at the front desk. This time would be easier for Nick - she didn't have to go through the entire sign-in process again.

She saw Nick before Nick saw her. Emma lingered by the door, quiet, watching Nick as she talked with the front desk guard. Nick was impeccably dressed, in her usual uniform of well-pressed slacks and blazer. Her badge was on her hip, with her gun and whatever else the detectives needed attached to the left side of her belt.

"Are you left handed?" Emma asked before she could stop herself.

Nick finished up at the desk and turned towards Emma. "I am," she said, patting her gun once. There was a smile on her lips that made Emma's stomach flip.

For a moment, for a second, she wanted to pull Nick into her arms and kiss her. Feel the safety and security she felt when in Nick's arms. But it wasn't the time, or the place.

"Where are we heading?" Nick's voice caught her off guard, dragging her back to reality.

"We keep all stuff left behind, for a period of time." Emma walked her through the common area, through a locked door and then out to the rear of the house. "It's kind of like our own set of storage areas."

Nick's eyebrows raised at the sight.

Emma smiled. They were coming up on what looked like four sheds, large enough that they could be bedrooms. And they had been, once upon a time. And could be, if required. But for now they held all of the possessions and furniture that belonged to past residents who no longer needed them.

"We sort them by year," Emma explained. "Some have files, some have furniture. Some have belongings."

"Do you own this place?" Nick asked, following her towards the sheds.

Emma stopped. "It's complicated." She didn't look back at her, instead walking towards the third shed that she knew held the personal knick-knacks that Rachel and Julia had left behind. "I inherited it from my Mom," she said. "Turned it into a domestic violence shelter after she died."

Nick made a thoughtful noise. "What was her name?"

Emma turned to look at her, a faint smile on her face. "Belle." Then she turned back to the shed, unlocking it with one of the keys on her keyring. "Both Rachel and Julia have some stuff in here," she said, pushing open the door. "They took most of their belongings with them, but some of it they stored here." Emma swallowed thickly.

"So this is stuff they left behind?" Nick looked around.

It was maybe twelve feet by fourteen feet. Not huge, but not small, either. Cardboard boxes lined the wall, up to five high. They were all sorted. "Here." Emma stood on her tip-toes to reach the top couple of boxes. Both Julia and Rachel were relatively recent, so their boxes were easier to get to.

She put the boxes down closer to waist level.

"Do you keep everything here?" Nick was watching her.

"Once six months has passed since leaving our charge we transfer them to our outside storage unit or destroy them, depending on whether or not they're sensitive," Emma said, finishing moving the boxes. "Here, these are Rachel's. You take them, I'll go through Julia's."

She waited until Nick started opening the boxes before she turned towards Julia's. She swallowed thickly, emotions threatening to overcome her. Here she was, looking through the last things Julia had left at Belle's House. Were they even going to show anything? After all, they'd already gone through what was in her house.

There were two boxes Julia had left behind, and some furniture in the fourth shed if they needed to look there. The first box was full of random papers, a few things that had been on her windowsill. The random little things that one accumulated when you lived in the same place for a while.

Emma started going through the papers, one by one. Most were random things. Flyers that had been distributed to Belle's House, notes Julia had written or journaled on. In therapy, both individual and group, the ladies were encouraged to write down their feelings, what they were going through.

She didn't let herself read most of them, just skimmed enough to know what the papers were. She didn't want to violate Julia's privacy. Even though she had been her therapist, there were boundaries she didn't want to cross. Not that it really mattered, now that she was dead.

She closed her eyes. Every time she thought about it, that pang of hurt ripped her heart in two. She had failed to protect her ladies.

"Did you keep records of voicemails?" Nick asked, drawing Emma out of her reverie.

Emma paused. "Probably." She lifted her head, thinking. "Approved people could call the front desk, we'd take notes."

"And you kept them?"

"Are you looking for anything in particular?" Where was she going with this train of thought?

Nick paused, deliberating. Emma could see it in her eyes. There was something she wasn't telling her.

Emma wanted to push her, but she turned her attention back to the box. She didn't want to risk pushing Nick too far, losing access to the investigation.

"We got information that an ex-boyfriend of Rachel's was leaving threatening messages for her," Nick said.

Emma thought back to Rachel's file. Yes, she had mentioned an ex.

Well, duh. They all had.

"I was wondering if you had any records of him calling, leaving threatening messages."

Emma shook her head. "We wouldn't allow those

types of calls," she said. "They'd be reported to the police and further monitored."

Nick nodded. She was skimming a few pieces of paper, but didn't speak.

Emma turned back to the box. She was about halfway through, mostly skimming pieces of paper. There was a small box, like the type that held index cards. She opened it, flipped through it. They were mostly business cards. Food places, all over the country.

But the last one - she stopped and looked at the last one.

Who are you looking for?
Private Investigator.
(999) 450-9755.

The area code was local.

She glanced at Nick, who had her attention focused on everything in front of her. Pulling out her phone, she googled the number. It led to a PI agency. *Find Me, INC. Specializes in finding, tracking, and reuniting.*

Interesting.

"What'd you find?" Nick's voice startled her.

"A business card for a PI firm," Emma said, showing it to her. "No name or address, though. Just a company name."

Nick took the card, examining it. She pulled an evidence bag out of the small kit she had with her, dropping the card in there and writing the date and time on it, as well as her initials. "It will do."

Emma studied her quietly, watching as Nick tucked the bag back into the kit. Nick had her eyebrows furrowed, her face intent in concentration as she picked through the boxes. She was reading papers more intently than Emma had been. She didn't have the personal connection.

"Were the women allowed to send letters?" Nick asked.

Emma nodded. "Twice a week."

Nick pulled out envelopes. Never sealed, but there was paper in them. "They're not even addressed."

Emma hesitated, but then pulled out one of the letters. It was addressed to Conner, from Rachel.

Dear Conner,

I know you won't forgive me. That's okay, I won't forgive you either.

It went on to recount a few incidents that she wouldn't forgive him for (no one deserved to be hit over the head with a beer bottle), and it ended with a cuss.

Emma's brow creased. What did she need forgiveness for? Leaving?

"Do you know where to find him?" Nick asked, her voice oddly calm.

Emma shook her head. "I think he does a physical job, like construction or something." She hated that it was so easy to lose track of which scumbag belonged to who. "I'd have to check my notes."

Nick nodded, then went back to the box. Emma watched her for a second, and then discreetly snapped a photo of the business card in its evidence bag. It wasn't her fault that Nick had left it near the top, right?

Eventually Nick straightened up, and sighed. "I think this is it," she said.

"What?" Emma blinked.

"I don't think there's anything else." Nick surveyed the boxes.

"What about Rachel's place?" Emma asked mulishly. Not that she was considering breaking into it. Again.

Nick's eyebrows raised and she stared at Emma. She seemed to be considering something, making a decision. "If you promise not to break into the crime scene, I'll take you there after we talk to Conner."

Emma just looked at her, startled. Then she smiled. "Thanks."

Nick's eyes shifted away, and there was a faint blush to her cheeks. "Just want to keep you from getting arrested, is all."

The quiet hung between them, their eyes locked. Emma's heart was racing, her cheeks flushed. Nick took a step closer, reaching up and cupping Emma's cheek.

Her hand was so warm against Emma's face, her body comfortably close.

Then Nick leaned in, her lips soft as they pressed against Emma's. A warmth started in her middle and radiated outwards, her lips moulding against Nick's. She wrapped an arm around her shoulders, pulling her closer.

Emma didn't know how long they kissed, but she knew she didn't want it to end. She didn't want a relationship, but at the moment, she definitely wanted to keep kissing Nick.

Eventually they broke for air. Emma was breathing faster, almost giddy. Nick looked half-worried and half-shy. It was an adorable look on her.

Emma reached over and tucked a short lock of hair behind Nick's ear.

Nick let out a soft laugh.

"It doesn't work quite as well on short hair," Emma said apologetically.

Nick chuckled, but didn't speak. "I should go," she said finally, breaking the silence. There was regret in her gaze now, but when she let go of Emma, Nick's fingers brushed her shoulder in an apology.

"You'd better call me!" Emma hurried after Nick, watching as the detective headed towards her police cruiser.

Nick raised a hand in acknowledgment, a smile on her face. "I will."

CHAPTER THIRTEEN

Friday, September 16th, 2016. 3:22pm.

Nick leaned back in her chair, staring up at the ceiling. She had spent most of the day searching through public records, looking for Rachel's ex-boyfriend. Connor. No last name. Why did nobody ever keep track of the last names? It would've made her life so much easier.

She regretted the thought the moment it left her head. Yes, it would've been easier for her.

"Anything to add to your whiteboard?" Spencer asked.

Nick sighed. "Not yet." She tapped her toes on the orthopedic thing on the floor. It was actually quite comfy. "I made a list of Rachel's former addresses," Nick said, pushing it towards Spencer.

He took it from her, looking at the documents. "She moved a lot."

Nick shrugged. She wasn't in a place to judge. "How do you want to split them up?"

"Let's start with the most recent," he said, pointing at one of the addresses. It also happened to be the closest one. "If she lived with him at some point, it's probably where they lived."

It wasn't a bad hypothesis.

And he was right. It was a small ramshackle house, with the blinds falling off and cracks in the walls. It was a dusty blue, as if it had been darker at one point but the paint had simply faded over the years.

She and Spencer exchanged a look, then headed towards the door. Nick's heart was racing, her body on alert. This was the scarier part of her job.

Spencer was the one who knocked on the door. "Battle Creek Police," he said, his voice loud and commanding.

The door cracked open, just enough that they could see some dirty hair and blue-eyes. Then it opened further. The man was in his late 20s, with scruffy black hair and a scraggly beard that hadn't been shaved in weeks.

"Connor?" Nick asked, her smile polite.

"Who wants to know?" Conner said, his voice gruff.

That bit always amused Nick. They had just introduced themselves as police. "My name is Detective

Tanner, and this is my partner Detective Jackson. We're with the Battle Creek Police Department."

Connor still stood in the doorway, not moving backwards.

"We'd like to come in," Nick said. "Just for a chat."

Connor studied them carefully, and then nodded, stepping back.

Nick went in first, keeping a close eye on escape routes. Her eyes searched his abode, but she always kept part of her attention on the potential suspect. She wasn't as weak as she looked, but men tended to over-estimate their own abilities and underestimate hers.

There were photos on the wall, photos of Rachel and Connor. They weren't that old, maybe six months to a year, by Nick's estimation. But, disturbingly, there had been marker drawn on the glass, giving Rachel a beard and horns. Like somebody would do in a high school yearbook. She turned to look at Spencer, and Spencer looked back at her. Neither of them said anything, and Connor didn't seem ashamed.

"What is this about?" Connor sounded more agitated.

"We just want to ask you a few questions about Rachel," Nick said, her voice pleasant.

There was a faint sneer on Connor's face. Not surprising, given the circumstances. "What about her?"

"We'd like to ask about the nature of your relationship." Spencer looked away from the photos, his face pointed, and back at Connor.

"It was nothing, and it's over, anyway," Connor said. He leaned back in his couch, seemingly more comfortable.

"Rachel's dead," Nick said flatly, watching his face intently. There was a flicker of shock, as if he was surprised they knew, but this information had not come as a surprise in itself. That was interesting.

"Oh." That was Connor's only reaction.

"What's your full name?" Spencer asked, drawing Connor's attention.

It was a good tactic, to push the pressure off him a little, but still keep him engaged.

"Connor Dawson," he said reluctantly.

"And you live here?" Nick asked, nonchalant.

There was the slightest hint of a snarl on his lips. "It's my place," he said.

"We have this registered to Rachel," Nick said, looking up from her notes.

Connor didn't say anything, but Nick could see the disgust. Was it his dislike for Rachel? Or was there something else?

"Where were you yesterday, around 3pm?" Nick asked when he didn't answer, her voice as amicable as she could make it.

He lifted his head slightly. "I was at home, watching

TV." He smirked. "Maury, to be exact. And he wasn't the father."

Nick had to wonder exactly what type of irony there was in that the potentially abusive ass watched Maury for fun. Still, she jotted it down, so she could check the TV listing.

"Would you be willing to come in tomorrow to talk to us?" It was easier to phrase things more neutrally, instead of automatically putting him on the defensive. He was definitely a person of interest, however.

Connor shrugged. "I can come after work."

"Where do you work?" Spencer asked, his voice friendly.

Connor shrugged. He didn't seem willing to answer.

"Would it be okay if we took a look around your house?" Nick asked, her voice casual as her eyes scanned the rooms around her.

Connor's eyes sharpened. "No." Then he smiled, something that seemed very out of place. "I'm packing, so things are messy."

"Oh, where you going?" Spencer asked.

"To Longview," Connor said, a smile on the corner of his lips. "Visiting a friend up there."

"I'd recommend staying in town," Spencer said, but he wasn't smiling.

"We'll see you at the station tomorrow," Nick said, moving towards the door.

Connor stood, ushering them out. "Bye," he said, shutting the door the moment they were out of it.

Nick and Spencer exchanged looks. Connor didn't seem particularly happy to be assisting their investigation. Not that that was surprising, given his apparent dislike of Rachel. Did he hate her enough to murder her? Or was the marker on the pictures just juvenile disdain?

"I'll talk to Emma, and get the records she has on him." That would be easy enough to do.

Spencer nodded in agreement.

WHILE NICK WAS DRIVING HOME, she started to yawn despite herself. She'd been up way too long, and sleep was essential.

Not that she was going to actually get any sleep. Her mind kept turning over what they had learned in their interviews, the relationships between Julia and Ryan and Connor and Rachel.

It wasn't just enough to identify who the killer was, they had to be able to prove it, too. The forensic lab was already at work helping identify what evidence they had, but it wasn't always useful until they had concrete suspects to test it against.

The killer hadn't left any DNA. Go figure.

Maybe she actually *would* try and get some sleep. A

power nap couldn't hurt, could it? Maybe she would call Emma, see if she discovered anything new.

But then they would have to talk about that kiss. Nick wasn't exactly certain she wanted to. Not that she regretted it – she definitely didn't.

She turned her attention reluctantly back to driving. And the case. She had other more important things to be focusing on that didn't include the feel of Emma's lips against hers. Besides, they were only going to see each other for the duration of the case. Once it was done, they would continue on with their normal lives. That was how it always was.

Guilt punched her in the stomach. How could she be kissing somebody new, after Sarah? She knew, theoretically, that it wasn't really that bad to move on, or meet somebody new, but it wasn't something she had been anticipating.

She pulled into her driveway, parking the car and turning it off. She sat there for a moment, her eyes closed. When was the last time she had slept? She didn't remember.

Grabbing the messenger bag that served as a purse, she got out of her car, slamming the door behind her. Then she stopped. She could see another car, parked across the street, with somebody in it.

The hackles on the back of her neck went up. It wasn't usual for someone to be there. That house was empty, and had been for a few months. And it wouldn't be the first time that she had been stalked by somebody. Although it would be the first time in Battle Creek.

Taking a deep breath, Nick leaned nonchalantly against her car, her hand hooked in her belt not far from her gun. She wanted to give them a chance and see what they would do.

She watched out of the corner of her eye as the person in the car lifted their head, looking in her direction. Nick's heart started beating faster.

She took a half step forward, the casualness dropping from her posture as her gaze focused in on the person getting out of the car.

"Do you ever take a break?" Nick looked at Emma, exasperated beyond belief. "I could have shot you."

"This counts as a break," Emma said, shutting her car door behind her. She had a purse over her shoulder, one of those tote bags that was currently in vogue. She was dressed in jeans and a blouse, with shoes that looked easy to walk in. "Besides, you said I could come over." She looked at Nick pointedly.

Nick tried not to think about the fact that her heart skipped a beat when Emma walked towards her. She was happy to see her, even after the fear that had momentarily railroaded her. When Emma got within touching distance, Nick hesitated. What kind of greeting did she want? Had Emma come to see her, or something else?

"Hi," Emma said, her voice and eyes soft. She stood there, looking at Nick. Nick, smiled, liking that she was two inches taller than Emma when she was in flats. Then again, she hadn't seen her in heels. "I didn't want to be alone." Emma's gaze flickered to Nick, then back into the distance.

Nick felt like she had been punched in the stomach, but she shoved it away. She knew that feeling. Sarah would have wanted her to be happy, not to be alone forever. And she wasn't forgetting Sarah, simply finding someone else. Wasn't that how it worked?

"What are you thinking about?" Emma asked, as Nick led the way to her front door.

"The case," Nick lied smoothly.

Emma nodded, her face solemn. "Have you guys found anything new?"

"I was wondering if you've gotten a hold of those phone records that you said you would?" Nick asked. "We found Rachel's ex-boyfriend; he's on the list." Nick paused, looking at her. "You're not sharing this, right?"

Emma shook her head. "What you say to me is in confidence," she said. Then her face became bland. "Besides, I wouldn't want to lose my access to the investigation."

Nick smiled despite herself. "So that's what I'm good for," she said with a wry expression. "just giving you information."

They were standing in front of the door, not quite in the house.

Emma smiled faintly and she reached out and touched Nick's hand. "More than that," she said softly. "But basically."

Nick let Emma hold her hand. She twined their fingers together, surprised at how much she liked the intimacy of the moment. It wasn't a hug, it wasn't a kiss, but she could've stood there holding Emma's hand forever.

Then a loud bay broke the silence. Emma looked at Nick, her eyebrows raised.

"That would be Lady Grey," Nick said.

"Let's go cater to her," Emma replied. "Otherwise she'll wake up the whole neighborhood."

Nick grinned, then unlocked the door.

Emma followed Nick inside the house, then followed her to the back where she let Lady Grey out of her kennel. Lady Grey ran around, barking excitedly as Nick headed back inside and prepared her dinner.

Emma leaned against the wall, watching the two of them. There was a smile on her face, and Nick's heart skipped a beat.

She forced it down. It wasn't like Emma really liked her. No, even Nick knew that was a blatant lie. She did like Nick. And Nick liked her a lot, really. Too much..

"How long have you had her?" Emma asked, dragging Nick out of her thoughts.

Nick glanced down at Lady Grey. "Couple years now," she said. "I've had her since she was a puppy."

Emma nodded.

Nick put down Lady Grey's bowl, standing up and watching her eat.

EMMA STUDIED NICK, thinking about the kiss and what had passed between them. She was still shaken after Julia's death, after Rachel's death. Two of her ladies had been brutally murdered.

Her face fell, and it was hard to keep a grip on her emotions. She wasn't going to cry, or anything like that. But it was hard to keep putting one foot in front of the other. Not that she would stop – she had an obligation to find the killer. But sometimes, life was exhausting.

"Something up?" Nick asked.

Emma considered the question. "It's been a long day," she said softly.

Nick nodded, understanding on her face. "We interviewed Rachel's boyfriend," she said. "But we're not close enough to identifying anyone as more than a person of interest yet."

"A person of interest being different to a suspect?" Emma asked.

Nick nodded. "It could be him, or it could be

another person that we haven't identified yet. We're interested in him, but not enough to focus our investigation solely in that direction."

"That mysterious person Julia was dating?" Emma asked.

Nick nodded. "Exactly."

When Lady Grey was done eating, she wandered out to the living room, hopping up on the couch and curling into a ball.

Emma just looked at Nick. "It's time for her post dinner nap," Nick said with a smile.

"Oh," Emma said with a grin. "I take it she naps a lot?"

"She's either napping, or running around like a crazy dog," Nick agreed.

They stood there in quiet contentment, not looking at each other and instead focusing on the dog. Emma was leaning against the wall, Nick against the counter.

Emma's heart fluttered, anxiety twisting her stomach. Were they going to talk about it?

"What are you thinking about?" Nick was looking at her.

It was ridiculous, what Nick's gaze did. Emma was a grown woman. A strong woman. She totally wasn't thinking about the feeling of Nick's lips against hers, nope.

"About you," Emma said honestly.

Nick smiled faintly.

Emma considered talking, considered baring her soul. But she wasn't certain it was the right time or place.

"Did you say something about getting some sleep?" Nick hid another yawn.

"Sleep is for the weak," Emma said with a smile.

"Well consider me one of the weakest," Nick snorted. She glanced at the couch, and then Emma. "You can sleep down here if you want to," Nick said. Then she hesitated.

Emma looked at her, curious. "Or?"

"Or," she said softly, "you could come sleep in my bedroom."

Emma looked at her, eyes alight.

"Not sex," Nick clarified quickly. "But I think it would be nice to be with someone right now." Nick looked away.

There was a strange feeling in the pit of Emma's stomach, one she didn't like. "That would be nice," she said softly, and she meant it. Sleeping next to someone else, especially someone as strong as Nick, would make her feel safe. She'd actually be able to sleep, not just close her eyes and think.

Nick was the one who led the way upstairs, Emma following. What was she going to wear? She had brought a purse, not pajamas.

Worst case, she could sleep in her underwear. It

wasn't like Nick hadn't seen a woman before. She'd been married, for heaven's sake.

Lady Grey followed them upstairs.

"Do you need pajamas?" Nick asked, leading her into the room off the top of the stairs.

"I haven't got any with me," Emma said. "But I can just sleep in my T-shirt," she added.

Nick pulled open a drawer, revealing a set of sweats, some legitimate pajamas, and anything else that Emma would've wanted. "You can use these, if you want," she said.

Part of the idea of smelling like Nick appealed to Emma, wearing her clothes. But that was ridiculous, or something.

She found herself reaching into the drawer and picking up a pair of sweats, and a T-shirt. It was better than sleeping in her bra, anyway.

Nick pointed to a door on the far side of the wall. "The master bedroom is through there," she said.

"Thanks," Emma said, holding the clothes to her chest and feeling awfully self-conscious. She took her clothes off, folding them and setting them to the side. Then she changed into Nick's clothes, delighting in the softness of the cotton against her skin. They were a little bit too big, given Nick's height, but they were warm and comfy and she was more than happy to sleep in them.

By the time she got back to the bedroom, Nick was

already tucked in one side. There was a TV on the far wall, and it was playing some cooking show quietly in the background.

"I sleep with the TV on," Nick said, an apology in her voice. "I hope that's okay," she said.

Emma blinked, but then nodded. She hesitated briefly, but crawled in her side of the bed. They were lying there, Nick on her back and Emma on her side. It was a little bit more awkward than Emma had expected it to be.

"You want to be the big spoon, or the little spoon?" Nick asked, turning on her side and propping her head up with an elbow.

Emma turned to look at her, a smile coming to her face. "Whatever you like," she said.

Nick chuckled. "That doesn't answer my question."

"It doesn't," Emma agreed. Then she turned around, putting her back towards Nick. That was her answer.

She felt Nick scoot closer to her, her warm body pressed against her. It felt like they fit, slotting together in just the right way.

Nick's arm wrapped over Emma's waist, pulling her snugly against Nick's body.

Emma liked it, she felt safe and secure. Even in the midst of what had been going on.

"How do you deal with this?" Emma asked before she could stop herself. She wasn't even 100% sure what she was referring to. The case? What they were doing?

They were two consenting adults, but Emma had never been very happy with ambiguity.

Nick pressed a kiss to Emma's hair. "You have to take things one day at a time," she said.

Emma nodded, understanding. She liked what they were doing, the simple intimacy of cuddling without the expectation of anything else. She was safe, she was secure, and she wouldn't rather be anywhere else.

"Get some rest," Nick murmured into her ear.

Emma did.

CHAPTER FOURTEEN

Saturday, September 17ᵗʰ, 2016. 7:23am.

Emma was the first to wake up. She pulled her phone out of her pocket, and laid there next to Nick, googling. She was checking her emails, trying to see if she'd been able to schedule Nick's surprise.

Not that she quite wanted to ruin the surprise before Nick found out what it was. She heard Nick yawn next to her, then roll over. Nick was stretching, an arm reaching up towards the backboard.

It was kind of cute, in Emma's opinion.

She turned to look at Nick, who was looking up at her.

"Good morning," Emma said.

"Morning." Nick looked for the clock. "What time is it?"

"About seven thirty," Emma said. Part of her

regretted not bringing a change of clothes. She would have to run by the house before they went and got breakfast.

"I should probably get to work," Nick said.

Emma looked at her. "Let's get breakfast first," she said.

Nick hesitated.

"We'll make it quick," Emma promised. And then we'll go to the appointment. That part she didn't say. Not yet.

THEY HEADED to a small breakfast joint that was locally owned. They were known for their crepes, and their creative use of ingredients.

They settled into a booth near the front, Nick dressed in street clothes and Emma dressed in whatever she could scrounge out of Nick's closet. Maybe if she kept this up, she'd be looking like a detective.

"Did you sleep well?" Nick asked, drinking some of her water that was on the table.

Emma nodded. It was the first time she had slept with someone in a long time, and she was quite certain she could get used to it.

Not that she wanted to get used to it. It was dangerous for her to get used to it.

"You?" Emma asked, wanting to laugh a little bit at the awkwardness of it all.

Nick smiled. They'd slept with Lady Grey between them, and it wasn't like she was the worst cuddling partner. But darn did she kick. "It was the first time I've slept with someone since Sarah died." Nick's eyes were far away.

Emma's heart tugged. "Oh." She didn't quite know what to say to that. I'm sorry? Thank you?

It wasn't like she had a lot of experience in that department either.

"I bet you miss her," Emma said softly. Her feet scooched forward, brushing against Nick's under the table.

"Every day," Nick said softly.

Emma hesitated. It was a personal question to ask, but they were having a moment. "How long has it been?"

Nick's smile was sad. "Three years. I came up here after Sarah died."

The waiter came by, and they both ordered. Peanut butter and banana crepes for Emma, and the strawberry cream cheese crepes for Nick.

"Have you ever been to France?" Nick asked.

Emma shook her head. "I don't travel much," she said with a wry smile.

Nick smiled, too. "The crepes they have here are just as good as those in France," she said.

"Is the chef French?" Emma asked.

"I think so," Nick said.

Emma smiled, delighting for a bit in the absurdity of the moment. Here they were, having breakfast, having just slept in the same bed last night. No sex, but snuggling counted. Defying all the u-haul lesbian stereotypes.

Yet all they were talking about was their breakfast crepes.

She didn't really want to ask, though. What they were doing.

Besides, it was just temporary. Once this case was over, she and Nick would go back to not crossing paths. That is, unless Nick needed to come to Belle's House for one reason or another. But she doubted it.

Emma let out a sigh.

"What are you thinking?" Nick asked.

Emma glanced at the clock on her phone. They still had 45 minutes. And they weren't very far away from their destination, so they didn't have to leave for a while either. "I don't know," Emma said finally.

Nick smiled wryly. "Why don't I believe you?"

Emma laughed. She checked the clock again, just in case it had changed.

Nick's eyes narrowed. "Why do you keep looking at the clock?" She paused. "Oh, are you late for work?" This time Nick glanced at the clock, as if she was worried about being late for her shift.

"No," Emma said evasively. "We kind of have an appointment."

"An appointment," Nick stared at her. "And what would that be?"

Emma dropped her fingers on the table, smiling at the waitress as their food was delivered. Taking a break from looking at Nick, she took a bite of her crepes, delighting in their taste. The light airy fluffiness of crepes, combined with the richness of the peanut butter and the sweet hint of banana. It was so worth the drive out here.

"Emma," Nick said, pointedly.

Emma tried to look innocent. "The business card?"

Nick narrowed her eyes.

"We have an appointment with Natalie the PI at 9:30," Emma said cheerfully.

Nick looked exasperated. "We talked about you not interfering in the investigation?"

"Technically I'm not interfering," Emma pointed out helpfully. "I'm simply pursuing this lead."

Nick smiled despite herself, and then took a bite of her own crepes. They were quiet for a bit while they were eating, but Emma liked the way their feet brushed under the table.

"What are your leads?" Emma asked, trying to keep her voice nonchalant. Even if it meant Nick was annoyed with her, she had to do everything she could to find out who had killed her ladies.

"We're following up with Rachel's ex-boyfriend," Nick said, taking another bite of her crepes. "He'd been leaving some nasty voicemails for her."

Emma nodded. "He called Belle's House once or twice, and been nasty to the staff. But we were able to block his number."

"How do you think he got it?" Nick frowned slightly.

"I don't know," Emma said. "We do the best that we can to keep things under wraps, but sometimes things escape us."

Nick nodded, thoughtful.

"Is there any way I could come with you?" Emma asked, a hopeful tone in her voice. "To interview the ex-boyfriend," she clarified.

Nick snorted. "Not a chance," she said. "But if you want, you can drop by the station later. Or by my house. We can talk about it."

Emma looked at Nick, and then smiled. Then she glanced at the clock, noting the time. "We should probably go."

Nick sighed. "Lead the way."

Emma had the address memorized. It was 1425 South Clark Lane. It wasn't the best part of town, but it wasn't the worst, either. Still, when Emma saw the building, she was wary.

It was made of bricks, but looked run down; some of the windows were starting to peel, and the paint was splotchy. It was obviously a set of suites, with a few lawyers, and then the building for Find Me, Inc.

"Who are we here to see?" Nick asked, looking expectantly at Emma.

"Her name is Natalie," Emma said. It was somewhat strange that she'd been willing to take Emma's call at three in the morning. Then again, she was a private investigator. Theoretically she'd been up doing something important at that time in the morning.

"Okay," Nick said.

"It is a bit sketchier than I expected," Emma admitted.

Nick chuckled, then shrugged. "I've seen a lot worse," she said. "Besides, the PIs never want to be noticed."

That was true.

They headed towards the suite, and Emma noted that instead of the usual glass, it was opaque, all but the door. And even that had a layer of stripes on it. "After you?" Nick asked, gesturing towards the door.

Emma smiled ruefully. Natalie was expecting them.

She pushed open the door, surprised to find out it was unlocked.

There was one small room and then another, with a barrier between them. "Natalie?" Emma asked, casting her eyes around.

A woman appeared out of a door that Emma hadn't noticed.

"Are you Natalie?" Emma asked, ignoring that it was an obvious question.

"Yes," Natalie said, her voice smooth. "Who am I talking to?"

"I'm Emma," she said, "and this is my friend, Detective Tanner."

Nick seemed amused by this.

"Now what exactly can I do for you?" Natalie asked, looking between the two of them. "You were rather vague on the phone."

"We found your business card in a recent homicide victim's belongings," Nick said, pulling a paper copy out of her pocket to show the PI.

Natalie looked between the two of them again. "Who?"

"Julia Rasmuth," Emma said softly. She probably should've waited for Nick to take the lead, but they were already there and she wasn't going to let something simple like a name keep her from finding out why Julia had been there.

"Oh." Natalie looked between the two of them. "What happened?"

"Julia was murdered," Nick said simply.

Emma felt the tug on her heart, the sadness that lingered there. There was another murder victim too, but they still weren't 100% sure it was related. Until then, Rachel's name should be kept out of this.

Natalie frowned slightly. "And you're here to find out what she hired me for?"

Nick nodded. "It would help our investigation."

Natalie nodded, heading past the door and into her office. "I keep my records in here," she said. "She came in about three months ago, wanting to be kept informed of someone's whereabouts."

"Any idea who it was?" Emma asked.

"Eric Sinclair," Natalie said promptly. "He is a local district attorney."

Nick's eyebrows shot up, and so did Emma's. They exchanged a look.

That would definitely qualify under what Julia had said, that the person who had hurt her was an important man. "Do you know the nature of the relationship between the two of them?

Natalie shook her head. "She was just interested in tracking his movements. She seemed scared, though."

"What did you find out?"

"He was rather boring," Natalie said. "Goes to work, goes home, spends time with his wife and son. We were going to have a meeting on the 13th at six, but Julia didn't show up."

So that was the meeting in her planner. "When was the last time you saw her alive?" Emma asked. She hated that she had to ask this.

"About two months ago," she said. "She came by for

an info gathering meeting, and then instructed me to continue watching him."

"How did she pay you?"

"Cash," Natalie said with a shrug. "It's pretty common in my line of work."

Where did she get that much cash? Emma frowned slightly. It wasn't often that someone came into the shelter with a lot of money, because if they had the resources, they had other places to go. Maybe she'd been saving it. She did have a job, after all.

"Is there anything else that you can tell us?" Nick asked.

"She did seem afraid of him," Natalie said thoughtfully. "And on one or two occasions, I saw her with bruises on her arms."

That was interesting, especially in Emma's opinion. Because that was after she had come to Belle's House, and when she'd been released to the halfway house. They did have a policy of no contact with the men or women that had sent them there, but there was also no guarantee that the women would adhere to that. Some didn't, and it restarted the vicious circle they had been caught in. But where did Rachel come into the whole situation?

"If there's any way you could get us the date and times of when you noticed the bruising, please send them to us." Nick handed her a business card.

Natalie nodded.

"Thank you," Nick said.

Natalie produced another business card, this one with her name on it. "If you need anything else, please let me know."

Nick took it. "Please call us if you think of anything that might be important."

"I will." Natalie looked between them. "Anything else?"

Emma shook her head, her mind spinning. Eric Sinclair? Who was that? An assistant district attorney. Was he the one that had killed Julia? They paused, right before they got to the door. Nick turned half back to look at Natalie, who was watching them leave. "You wouldn't, perhaps, have met with this woman, either?" She produced a photo of Rachel, showing it to Natalie.

Natalie studied her for a moment, and then shook her head. "She hasn't come by the office before."

Nick nodded, tucking the photo back in a file. "Thanks," she said, leading them out of the door.

They stopped not far from Nick's car, not speaking but thinking instead. Emma's mind was spinning. Obviously, they needed to go check out this guy next.

"You need to go back to Belle's House," Nick said, her voice soft to cushion the impact of her words.

Emma frowned at her. "I want to go check out this Sinclair guy," she argued.

"I've already pushed boundaries far enough letting you come with me here," Nick said, her voice pragmatic. "Go back to Belle's House, and I'll let you know when we find anything out."

Emma hesitated. She did have a double memorial to plan now. Guilt tugged at her at the thought. "Okay," she said softly.

Nick nodded. "I'll give you a ride to your car," she said.

Emma hopped in the passenger seat, reaching out to squeeze Nick's hand. "Thank you," she said, and she meant it. Nick had gone out on a limb, letting her into as much of the investigation as she had. Emma didn't want to overstep, but she also wanted to find out what happened to her ladies.

Nick started the car, not looking Emma. "You could always come by later," Nick said. She fidgeted a tiny bit, looking to the side. "If you want to."

Emma's stomach fluttered. Whatever it was, it was too early to define it, but it did make her happy. "That works," she said, teasing. Nick smiled, and headed back towards Emma's car.

CHAPTER FIFTEEN

Saturday, September 17ᵗʰ, 2016. 1:27pm.

Nick parked at the station, getting out of her car and taking her keys and bag with her. She needed to talk to Spencer, update him on what she had learned while talking to Natalie. Then she had to call the DAs office.

That was the downside of dealing with assistant district attorneys; they were very difficult to get hold of because they were often in cases or working outside of the office interviewing potential witnesses. Still, there was a central secretary who might be able to get hold of him if she couldn't reach him directly. Even if it was the weekend.

She dialed Eric Sinclair's number as she walked inside, listening to it ring. There was no answer on his line. She would call the secretary's number once she was at her desk.

Nick pushed her way into the police station, nodding to Nancy, the police secretary as she headed inside. They also had that meeting with Connor, but it could always be moved. Theoretically.

"Welcome back," Spencer said, a wide grin on his face.

Nick chuckled wryly. "I may have found another suspect."

Spencer sighed. "That's the last thing we need."

"But this one might actually be guilty," Nick said with a wink. It was hard when they had several suspects and very limited ways to narrow them down. "Any word from forensics?"

The hair found in Rachel's condo is obviously dog hair," he said. "Further tests are being run to see whether or not the DNA is similar to Quentin's."

Nick blinked, unable to place the name.

"Kylie's dog," Spencer said. "It would allow us to tell whether or not he was in the room."

That was useful. "What time is Connor's interview?"

Spencer glanced at the clock. "20 minutes," he said. "If he shows up."

Nick glanced at him. "Skeptical?" She asked.

Spencer smiled wryly. "Very."

Nick filled him in very quickly on what had happened with Natalie.

"Next time, call me first." Spencer winked. "Don't go stealing all the cute ladies."

Nick rolled her eyes. "Emma was the one who tricked me," she said.

Spencer chuckled. "So, it's worth following up on this Eric."

"I'll call into the secretary and get a meeting set up with him." They didn't know enough about him to do a surprise meeting, or to get any type of warrant. For now, they would be civil. It was the best chance of getting him to talk about whatever it was that had happened.

"I'll go check on Connor," Spencer said, heading out of the room.

Nick headed towards her office, dialing the number.

"Hello?" The secretary answered the phone.

Absently, Nick wondered how much they must be paying her to work on Saturdays. "I'm looking for assistant district attorney Eric Sinclair?" Nick said, settling a notepad near her so that she could write if she needed to.

"He's currently out working on a case," the secretary said. "Can I take a message?"

"This is Detective Nick Tanner with the Battle Creek Police Department," Nick said. "I'm interested in talking to him about a case that he was involved in," she said, keeping it as generic as possible. She didn't want to give him time to prepare an alibi or to think about his story ahead of time, if he was guilty.

"Do you have a number you can be reached at?" The secretary asked.

Nick gave her office number. "Any idea what time he'll be back in the office?"

"Oh, probably not until Monday."

Nick bit back a sigh. It wasn't the secretary's fault that lawyers didn't work as much as the cops did. Nick nodded, even though the secretary couldn't see her. "Thank you," she said.

The secretary hung up without a goodbye. Nick raised her eyebrows at the phone, but then shrugged it aside. She had better things to worry about.

Not until Monday. Go figure. What about dropping by his home? She'd have to run that by Spencer.

She turned her attention to updating some of the paperwork, gathering the witness statements and documenting what Natalie had said. Later she would need to go back to the PI agency, and get Natalie to sign paperwork affirming what she'd said. But that could wait.

Spencer popped his head back in the pod, his face grim.

"What?" Nick asked, looking up from her work.

"Police were doing a routine check of his neighborhood and they found Connor's home empty," Nick said.

Nick blanched. "Empty?"

"As if nobody lived there," Spencer said, frowning. "He must've fled."

Damn it. Not that fleeing automatically meant he was guilty, but it didn't necessarily mean anything good, either. She paused, thinking over their prior interview. "Didn't he mention relatives in Longview?"

Spencer nodded. "I already have one of the patrol officers looking into it," he said. "But there's no guarantee he went there."

"Could he be heading towards the station?" Nick asked.

Spencer let out a snort. "Maybe in a fantasy world," he said.

Nick had to agree. It was rare that criminals voluntarily showed up for their interviews.

"Let's head toward the aunt and uncle's house," he said. "Just in case."

Nick nodded. She drove.

When they got there, there were three cars in the driveway. Would they seriously get that lucky? She and Spencer got out of the patrol car, heading up towards the front door. She was the one that knocked, since she looked less threatening. The door creaked open. "Hello?"

The lady was probably mid 50s, maybe mid 60s, and a little bit hostile looking. Her eyes were sharp and they were fixed directly on Nick.

"We're looking for Connor?" Nick said politely, flashing her badge. "We just want to talk to him."

"That boy ain't here," a male voice shouted from inside the room. It sounded too old to be Connor so maybe it was his uncle.

Out of the corner of her eye she watched Spencer duck off to the side, but kept her attention on the person in front of her. "We just want to talk to him," she said, keeping her voice even.

"You want to take him away," the aunt said.

"If he is guilty, then yes," Nick said honestly.

Then there was a shout, and the sound of some pots breaking. A few seconds later, Spencer came out from behind the house, Connor in front of him, his hands cuffed behind his back. "He was fleeing out the back," Spencer said.

Nick winced a little bit inside. Cuffing him like that wasn't going to endear them in the eyes of his aunt and uncle. They'd be less likely to talk, if they could offer anything.

"We just want to talk to you," Nick said, looking at Conner.

Connor laughed at her.

"Why were you running?" Nick asked.

Connor looked at her as if she was stupid. "You're going to lock me up for killing that bitch and I didn't do anything!"

Nick and Spencer exchange glances. "While that

happens sometimes, we try not to let it happen," Nick said mildly. "Why did we find threatening voicemails from you on Rachel's phone?"

Connor glared at the ground. "She left me."

"Please hold on, ma'am." Nick caught sight of the aunt sneaking up behind them.

The aunt scowled.

"If you assault an officer, you'll get in trouble." Spencer was the one that spoke.

"It's okay, Auntie." Connor spoke. "Go back inside."

The aunt ruffled up to her full height, maybe five feet, and then stomped back inside, muttering under her breath.

But Connor hadn't spoken to his aunt with any amount of vitriol, or anger, that Nick would've expected. If he had been angry enough to murder Rachel, commit overkill and commit a passion-based murder, where was the passion?

"Do you have an alibi?" Spencer asked, "for where you've been today?"

Connor jerked his head towards his aunt and uncle inside. "I've been here since this morning," he said.

"You know they could be charged with obstruction of justice," Nick pointed out.

Connor's eyes hardened. "You don't touch them." His voice was almost a snarl.

Nick and Spencer exchange glances. Here was a glimpse of the aggression they been expecting. "So why did you leave those messages on Rachel's voicemail?" Nick asked again, her voice nonchalant. Maybe if she kept asking, he would actually answer honestly.

Connor glared at her. "Because she was a bitch."

How flattering of him. "Why now?" she asked, pragmatic. "Why not when she actually left? Why over the last couple of months?

Connor bristled. "She was a bitch. The whole time."

"She wouldn't take you back?" Nick guessed.

His face went an ugly shade of red. "Fag," he muttered, his face drooping.

The pieces fell into place. "You found out she was dating a woman." She didn't say the name, just in case Connor was going to target her instead.

Connor seemed to deflate a little bit. "Yeah," he admitted. "I could see her leaving me for another man," he said. His face darkened. "But a woman? That's a blow to a guy's ego."

That was something Nick didn't really agree with, but there were points she was going to argue and points that she wasn't.

"So when did your stalking start?" Nick asked, careful to keep the judgment out of her voice. She didn't want him to clam up and stop speaking, she wanted him to stay conversational.

Besides, they still needed to do elimination prints. His weren't in the system, which meant he hadn't been convicted of a felony.

"Will you come with us to the station to do elimination prints?" Nick asked, looking over her small notepad.

Connor visibly hesitated. "How far away?" he asked.

Nick consulted her phone, thoughtful. "We'll get you home in time for dinner." That was, as long as he answered their questions. "As long as you're honest with us."

Connor looked back and forth between her and Spencer. She could see on his face that he was aware he didn't have a choice. "Fine."

CHAPTER SIXTEEN

He stood there, watching. He was far enough away, half hidden behind a tree, that they couldn't see him. He had seen the curly-haired lady with Julia before. She was the one that had taken Julia away. The other lady, he knew through others. She was a detective, a transplant. She wasn't local. She wouldn't understand him.

How many pieces had they put together? Was he going to need to do something drastic? That seemed like the best option. After all, he couldn't get caught. There was too much at stake.

He pulled out his phone, dialing his brother's number. "Jeffrey?" He needed to hear his brother's voice, hear his brother's reassurance. "What should I do?

"You know what to do," Jeffrey's voice came to the phone, self-assured.

He took a deep breath, hanging up the phone and tucking it into his pocket. He did know what to do. He knew exactly what he needed to do, and he was going to do it.

Preventative measures were a very good idea.

CHAPTER SEVENTEEN

Monday, September 19ᵗʰ, 2016. 9:22am.

Nick sat at her desk, her feet up on the thing that Spencer's child had given her. She had several websites open and several case files right in front of her. She was doing all the research that she could on Eric Sinclair, trying to figure out who he was and how he was tied into this case. He was married, mid 30s and had been an assistant district attorney with Clark County for several years. He had graduated from a midrange law school, with middle of the range grades.

He seemed the epitome of 'perfectly ordinary'.

He had no siblings or extended family. It was just him, his wife, and their son. His wife was a trust fund baby, whereas he didn't come from money. Was it an affair? Or was Julia having him followed for some other reason?

Nick highly doubted that, but it was something that had to be ruled out.

She heard the phone ring, picked it up and tucked it to her ear. "Hello?"

"We just received a 911 call about a woman bleeding at Belle's House," the operator said grimly. "Hit over the head with some sort of blunt object."

Nick's heart stopped. "What?"

"Curly hair, 5'6", they think she's the owner, Emma Stevens," the operator continued.

Already Nick was throwing her belongings into her bag, the case files and everything else. She had a few hours before they were set to meet Eric. She should go and try and keep Emma from getting into more trouble.

Okay, and she just wanted to make sure she was okay.

"Where are they taking her?" Nick asked, grabbing her keys and heading out of the police department. The operator quickly named Jordan's hospital.

Relief surged through Nick. Jordan was one of the lead physicians in the ICU, but Nick knew the hospital's reputation overall. Surely the emergency care unit would take good care of Emma.

Instead of asking for more information, Nick hung up the phone and got in the car. She had to see Emma. She had to make sure she was okay. And odds were it was related to the case somehow. Otherwise it was a pretty big coincidence.

After a few years on the police force, Nick didn't believe in coincidences.

She dialed Jordan's number, waiting for it to connect via Bluetooth.

"Nick?" Jordan answered on the third ring.

"Hey, are you at the hospital?" Nick kept her focus on the road, no matter how much her attention wandered.

"Of course." Jordan sounded amused.

"Emma's heading to the hospital with a head wound, can you go check on her?" It wasn't Nick didn't trust the ER doctors, but it was Emma. Nick worried.

"Got it." Jordan hung up her end of the line.

Nick threw her phone on the passenger seat, her stomach churning. She didn't like the ambiguous wording the operator had used. "Found down". Was she conscious? Comatose? Or was she fine? Well. She definitely wasn't fine, but there were accidents that could be better rather than worse.

Nick sped on her way to the hospital, grateful that she avoided getting a ticket. Not that a fellow cop would necessarily have given her one, but it was a conversation she was glad to avoid. Parking, she headed straight to the ER, grateful for the badge on her hip that would get her inside. Even though this visit was both personal *and* professional.

"I'm looking for Emma Stevens?" Nick said, flashing her badge. "I'm Detective Tanner, it's related to a case."

Technically it was, and it wasn't a lie.

The nurse at the front desk quickly studied her badge, then jerked her head towards the back. "Bay three," she said, turning back to the chaos of the ER around them. Ducking through the sterile front doors, Nick headed straight for number three. It wasn't too far, just off to the right side. It was hidden by a sheet, with a small see-through area. She could see Emma inside, laying on the bed.

She pushed open the curtain, stepping in. There was a doctor sitting on a stool next to Emma, forceps in her hand. She was gently dabbing a sponge on Emma's forehead.

"Hi," Nick said softly, but she grimaced at the word. She turned to the doctor, more comfortable with that element. "I'm Detective Tanner, a friend of Emma's." She showed her the badge.

The doctor nodded. Nick didn't recognize her, but she was a nice-looking woman, with friendly eyes and greying hair. "She's getting stitches, then a few scans."

Nick searched Emma with her eyes. She could see the clotted blood in her curly hair, see the places where it had dripped down onto her shoulder. Her light-colored shirt was now stained with rust color.

Before Nick realized it, her heart was starting to

race, her adrenaline surging. She wanted to go find whomever had hurt Emma and hurt them back.

"I'm okay," Emma said, apparently cluing into Nick's flash of emotion.

Nick glanced at the doctor, who moved her hands away from Emma as she did something doctorly with the stitching kit. Throwing caution to the wind, Nick stepped forward and hesitated barely a second before she kissed Emma, her hand tenderly cupping Emma's cheek, careful of the wound on her head.

When Nick pulled back, Emma's eyes were shimmery.

"I'm okay," Emma said, but her voice was weaker.

"I was worried," Nick said softly.

Both closed their eyes for a moment, sharing the intimacy. Nick focused on breathing in and out. She could smell Emma underneath the acrid, bitter tang of blood. Emma was okay. She was breathing. She was safe.

The doctor coughed politely, and Nick kissed Emma one last time before she straightened up.

"What's the last thing you remember?" Nick asked, shifting back into detective mode.

Emma sighed. "They hit me as I was leaving Belle's House. Never heard or saw a thing." She sounded bitter.

Nick glanced at the clock. Between the driving, and

the talking, she had another 30 to 45 minutes to spend with Emma before she had to leave.

"What are you watching the clock for?" Emma asked, her voice suspicious.

"We have an interview at eleven," Nick said honestly.

Emma's face brightened up, even if she grimaced as the thin syringe slid into her skin.

"Lidocaine," the doctor said. "She needs stitches."

Nick's stomach banged in sympathy. She couldn't imagine that would be any fun. And where was Jordan? Probably putting out a fire in the ICU. Go figure. "How many?"

The doctor shrugged, injecting lidocaine into a few more places. "Six, eight. We're not sure."

Emma looked at Nick, careful not to tilt her head. "Who are you interviewing?"

Nick didn't answer.

"It's him, isn't it?" Emma narrowed her eyes, which seemed to cause some pain.

At least she didn't name him.

Nick sighed. "Yes, it is," she said.

"Can I come?" Emma asked, trying not to move as the doctor slid the stitching material into her head.

"If you're cleared," Nick said without thinking. Between the stitches and the probable concussion, there was no way Emma was going to get approval to go anywhere.

Theoretically.

The curtain guarding the bay shifted to the side, and Jordan walked in. She was a tall, thin woman, with short brown hair. She smiled at Nick, and drew her into a hug. "How's she doing?"

"She's being a champ," the doctor said.

"As stoic as Nick," Jordan said with a chuckle, shaking her head. There was a smile on her face. "You're in good hands," she informed Nick. The doctor doing the stitches smiled and turned back to her work.

Nick looked at her. "Which one?"

Jordan grinned. "Both of you."

Nick rolled her eyes, but part of her was touched. Jordan really did care about her.

"What's the plan of attack?" Jordan turned her attention to the doctor currently doing Emma's stitches.

"MRI, maybe a CT." The doctor was focused on the stitches. Jordan was nodding, which was reassuring to Nick. It meant that she agreed this was the right treatment plan.

"She was hit that hard?" Nick asked.

"Better safe than sorry, even though she didn't lose consciousness," the ER doctor answered. "Probably some sort of baseball bat or something."

Nick swallowed thickly, thinking back to Rachel's autopsy report. That would fit the instrument that the coroner had described. This could be the link. Was it enough to confirm that Emma's attack was related to one of the murders? Or was it just coincidence?

"I need to go talk to Spencer," Nick said, nodding to the doctors.

"Go," the doctor said with a shooing motion. "We'll be fine," she added.

"They gave me the good drugs," Emma said with a wink.

Nick smiled despite herself, then nodded and quietly left the ER. She dialed Spencer, listening to her phone ring.

"Hello?" he said, his voice tired on the other end.

Had he been up too long? She didn't even know what his schedule was at the best of times, not that they really adhered to one when they were working on an active case.

"Emma's been attacked," she said, her voice grim.

Spencer let out a surprised noise. "What happened?"

Nick shook her head, even though he couldn't see her. "They think she was hit with a baseball bat of some type," she said. "It fits the description the ME gave me of what could have caused the blunt trauma injuries on Rachel."

Spencer whistled. "Where are you?"

"At the hospital where she is," Nick said, aware she should have been feeling sheepish but not actually sheepish at all.

Spencer chuckled.

"I'm worried about leaving her alone," Nick started, hesitant.

"We have the Sinclair interview at eleven," Spencer said.

"Emma might be useful," Nick hesitated, "If she's medically cleared."

There was silence on the other end of the call, and for a moment Nick wondered if she was crossing the line. It was a lot to ask of another officer, especially in a small unit such as theirs. Emma was a civilian, and she was personally attached to these cases. Could she remain objective?

Could she help them with anything that they couldn't find for themselves?

"How bad is the damage?"

"She'll need six or eight stitches," Nick said, thinking of the doctor.

"If the doctor clears her, then bring her along. If the doctor doesn't release her, we'll get a patrol officer to keep watch over her at the hospital." Spencer's voice was firm. "Whatever's going on, we need to get to the bottom of it, and fast."

"Thanks," Nick said, her voice genuine. She hung up the phone, heading back into the ER.

When she came back in, the stitches had been finished, and the doctor was taping the gauze patch to her forehead. Jordan was still leaning against the drapes, watching Emma with a curious look.

"What's that for?" Nick asked suspiciously, looking at Jordan.

"She's nice," Jordan said purposefully.

Nick tried not to scowl, but she couldn't stop the corners of her lips from turning down into a disapproving frown. "Yes," she said instead. Nick turned her attention towards the doctor. "Any verdict yet?"

"I say she's cleared to leave once the scans are done, as long as they come back clear," the doctor said, sitting back up on her stool. "I'm assuming she'll be monitored for the next 12 to 24 hours?"

Nick nodded. "She'll be with my partner and I." She paused. "My detective partner." Better clarify. Better safe than sorry.

Jordan grinned. "I'll see you later," she said, waving to both Nick and Emma before she headed out of the room.

Nick glared at her retreating form, ignoring the hint of the blush that rose in her cheeks. She sighed. "Once the scans are done, we can leave."

Emma grinned.

NICK WASN'T SURPRISED, when Eric walked through the door, to realize that she recognized him. Several of the ADAs came to their department, since they were in charge of prosecuting a lot of their cases. She and

Spencer walked Eric down the hallway into one of the interrogation rooms. It was one of the nicer ones, since he was only here for questioning. Emma was hanging out in the control room, watching through a two-way mirror. Nick still felt some uneasiness around this, but she needed to keep an eye on Emma, and it was the closest way to do it.

"Sorry about our surroundings," Nick said, "we're having our client rooms remodeled. The money has finally come through in the budget".

Eric smiled, and he was charming when he smiled. He was tall, taller than she had expected, with short, shaggy black hair and bright brown eyes. He was dressed in his usual court clothes, a nice suit.

"Why am I here?" Eric asked, looking between Nick and Spencer.

"I was wondering if you happen to recognize this woman?" Spencer asked, passing a photo of Julia across the table.

Eric's gaze lingered on her, and a slight furrow formed between his brows. "Is she okay?"

"So you recognize her?" Nick asked.

Eric let out a sigh. "Yes," he said softly. "She worked in the diner near the courthouse."

"What was her name?" Nick asked, as if she had forgotten.

"Julia." The word was barely audible.

Excitement stirred inside Nick. "Did you talk to her much?"

"She was a sweet, beautiful girl," Eric said, his gaze flickering between Nick and Spencer. "Did something happen to her?"

"She was murdered," Spencer said, his voice solemn. "Where were you on the night of the 13th?"

"I was at home with my wife and son," Eric said, a slight frown on his face. "Why?"

"Have you seen this business card before?" Nick slid a copy of Natalie's business card across the table. For the second time, Eric picked something up and looked at it.

"No," he said, looking it over. "I haven't seen this before."

"This is a Private Investigatory agency that Julia asked to follow you," Spencer said affably. "Why would she do that?"

Eric let out a sigh. "I was hoping this wouldn't have to come to light," he said, regret in his words. "I dallied with Julia once, and I'm afraid she became quite obsessed with me."

If Nick had heard it once, she had heard it a million times. "Dallied?"

"Went to a hotel once, and had sex," Eric said. "But I came clean to my wife and swore to never do it again."

"Then why was Julia having you followed?" Spencer asked, looking confused.

"She became a bit infatuated, I'm afraid." Eric sounded regretful. "She kept calling, and calling. Even showed up at my workplace one day."

Nick tapped her finger on her elbow, thinking. Her eyes scanned the room, intensely observing him. She caught sight of the pet hair on his slacks. Even attorneys couldn't always keep their clothes clean.

Wait – that clicked in her mind. Kylie had mentioned her dog. Ryan had had dog hair on his pants. "Do you have a pet at home?" Nick asked, her voice casual.

Eric chuckled, glancing down at his slacks and trying to brush the pet hair off. "We have a mini Aussie," he said. "She gets a lot of hair everywhere."

Nick studied him for a moment, not entirely convinced but having no evidence to the contrary. It was easy enough to verify after the interview.

"She did have an ex-boyfriend that caused trouble," Eric said thoughtfully.

Spencer looked surprised, and inwardly Nick envied his acting skills. "What happened?" Spencer asked.

"We were having lunch, and he appeared, swearing at Julia and causing quite the scene." Eric's lips curled up in distaste.

"When was this?" Spencer asked, pretending to consult his notes.

Eric seemed to realize his misstep. "It was the day we went to the hotel," he said, his body slightly stiff.

"Can you walk through that day for me?"

"We met up at the diner, went and had lunch, and then went to the hotel and had sex for the rest of the day."

Nick could see a glimmer of contempt in his eyes. But she wasn't sure what it was for. The police? Julia?

Still, she wrote his name and underlined it, careful to keep it hidden. He didn't replace Connor and Ryan, but he was a suspect.

"Is it okay if we search your office, car and home?" Nick asked, hoping he would agree so that they wouldn't have to apply for a search warrant. They definitely didn't have enough forensic evidence to tie him to anything.

"You can search my office and my car, but I request that my home not be disturbed. I do not want to upset my wife."

Nick nodded. "How old is your son?"

"He's nine," Eric said proudly. "Head forward on his soccer team."

Nick nodded thoughtfully. "Are you willing to take us to your car?"

Eric led the way.

"You should go home," Spencer said, looking at Nick instead of following him.

Nick glanced over towards Emma, in the hidden room. "Forensics," she started.

"I'll take care of it." Spencer waved a hand at her. "I'll let you know if we find anything."

Nick hesitated, then nodded. "Thanks." She hadn't had much of a chance to talk to Emma during the actual interrogation, but she was curious to hear Emma's impressions. Of all their leads, she had spent the most time with the victims.

But if Eric was Julia's killer, why would he kill Rachel? Why risk drawing attention to himself?

"Let's get you home," Nick said, heading towards Emma.

Emma had a stubborn set to her lips.

Nick sighed. "Not to sleep, but so we can get some work done."

Emma's face relaxed. She grinned. "Better."

CHAPTER EIGHTEEN

Monday, September 19ᵗʰ, 2016. 4:51 pm.

Emma got in the passenger seat of Nick's car, her head throbbing. She had tried to stay strong, but now she was starting to get tired. After the interview with Eric Sinclair, her head was spinning in circles. What was the truth? How much was he lying about? Because if there was one thing she was certain about, that was it: he was lying. About what, though?

"Ok if I take you to my place?" Nick asked, glancing at her.

Emma nodded. It was safer, she guessed. And probably closer. "Lady Grey there?"

Nick started the car. "Jordan dropped her off a little bit ago," she said.

"How did you meet her?" Emma asked, the pain making her curious for a distraction.

"She grew up here," Nick said. "Left for medical training, but came back. We became good friends after that."

It wasn't entirely an answer to her question, but it was good enough.

She spent the rest of the car ride with her head against the window, wincing every time the car hit a bump.

At the house, Nick helped her out of the car.

Emma didn't like feeling like an invalid, or feeling weak. She turned to look at Nick, who was watching her. "Do you need anything?" she asked.

"The doctor gave me some painkillers." Emma glanced around, not sure where she had left them.

Nick found them and brought them to her with a glass of water.

"Thanks," Emma said, popping the pill in her mouth and taking a sip of water. Her mouth was dry, and the pill stuck to her tongue, letting its bitter taste seep into her mouth. She grimaced.

They were quiet for a moment, and then Nick looked at her. "You should probably get some sleep."

Emma frowned. "What about work?"

"You need to rest," Nick said.

"But Julia's killer, Rachel's killer - they're still out there."

"So is your attacker." Nick's voice was stern. "You need to rest so that you can recover."

Emma deflated, the throbbing in her head intensifying. She hated what Nick was saying, but she knew it was true, too.

"You take the bed, I'll take the couch." There was a note of hesitation in Nick's voice, but Emma wasn't sure why.

Emma paused. Was Nick asking something more? Was she not comfortable with it? The kiss in the ER had sort of insinuated otherwise. Besides, they had already slept in the same bed once. It was just a comfort thing, right? Not a couple thing? Or, you know. Whatever sort-of friends did when they kissed and whatever.

Yay for loopy painkiller thoughts.

A ringing sound broke the silence, and Emma cringed at the way the tinny noise pierced her head.

"Sorry." Nick pulled her phone out of her pocket, silenced it, and put it on the small table near the door. "How's your head?"

Emma snorted, then winced as the gesture made her hurt even more. "Pounding," she admitted.

"Here." Nick looped her arm around Emma's shoulder and propped her up as they headed up the stairs. She had apparently made a decision, and it was one that Emma agreed with.

She didn't want Nick to be on the couch. She wanted Nick to be with her, to keep her company, to be that safe and secure presence that grounded her. She liked being around Nick, her dedicated stubbornness, her tenacity. Her determination to track down whoever was doing wrong and to catch them.

To track who had killed people Emma cared for.

Nick pushed open the bedroom door, helping Emma inside.

Lady Grey, however, had other plans.

Emma felt a furry rump hit the back of her calves and her knees buckled suddenly, dropping her to the floor.

Nick fell to the ground with her, her arms around Emma to protect her.

It kept Emma's head from hitting the ground, and for that, she was eternally grateful.

When Emma looked at Nick, to thank her, she found they were almost nose-to-nose, kneeling, at eye-level.

Emma's heart started racing, and the thudding in her head disappeared into the background. Her breath was coming shorter, sharper, and all she wanted to do was lean forward and kiss Nick.

"Ouch!" Nick was the one that yelped this time as the furry cannonball of Lady Grey bounded between the two of them, trying to lick both of their faces at the same time and get as much attention as she could.

Emma blinked, then broke into giggles, scratching Lady Grey behind her ear and getting rewarded with a few licks to the face and a wagging tail. She couldn't help but smile, watching as Nick scratched Lady Grey's rump and the dog's wiggling escalated in fervor.

"She's going to explode," Emma said.

Lady Grey barked between licks, then tucked her head next to Emma's neck.

Emma stroked the velvety head, the soft ears. She had never had a dog before, never really considered herself a dog person, but after meeting Lady Grey, she wasn't sure she could imagine life without one.

"We should get off the floor," Nick said, her voice soft.

Emma's knees agreed. "Not sure I can." The throbbing in her head was back, settling in as a dull roar near the back of her skull.

"I can help." Nick moved into a crouch.

It was awkward, not because of Nick, but because of the beagle who was determinedly inserting herself into every possible space she could fit in.

Emma smiled.

Eventually Nick had her standing up again, even though Emma was probably leaning into her more than was required. She liked being close to Nick, feeling the warmth of her body, smelling the slightly citrus scent of her skin.

"Bed," Nick said, her voice husky. Then her cheeks flushed. "I meant we should go to bed. Uh, go to sleep, I mean."

Emma arched an eyebrow, enjoying Nick's flustered

behavior. Then her face shifted, becoming more solemn, meeting Nick's eyes.

Nick looked back at her, and the moment hung between them. Even Lady Grey seemed to respect it - although with any luck, she was off somewhere getting into trouble.

Then Emma started leaning forward, and Nick didn't stop her.

When their lips touched, it wasn't like the movies. There weren't fireworks, no. What it was, was way better. The feelings sparked down her body, leaving her warm and flushed as her lips opened against Nick's. Need pulsed through her, and she was hot, too hot.

"What are we doing?" Nick asked against her lips, between open-mouthed kisses.

"Kissing," Emma said back, tilting her head to the side and sliding her hand into Nick's short hair. "And maybe more."

The door creaked, and both of them froze, looking in its direction, just in time to see Lady Grey's tail disappearing out the door.

Nick looked exasperated. "Who knows what she's going to get into."

"Is that really your focus right now?" Emma lifted her eyebrows. Her head hurt, she was sore from the fall on the floor, but she pushed all of that out of her mind. Her focus was on Nick, and Nick only.

"We shouldn't do this," Nick said, but she was staring at Emma's lips.

"Why?" Emma challenged. "You like me, I like you." She shrugged. "It doesn't have to be anything special."

Nick let go of her, then caught her wrists, the grasp gentle. "But it is," she said softly. Her face was deadly serious.

Emma met her eyes, ignoring the prickle of heat emanating from Nick's hands on her. She swallowed thickly, trying to think of something to say. "I'm not good at this," she admitted.

"Neither am I," Nick agreed. "I work too much, I'm stubborn, married to the job…" Her voice trailed off.

"But I like those things about you," Emma said without thinking.

Nick looked at her, a smile on her face now.

The conversation was getting a lot more serious than Emma had intended. Her stomach felt like it was tied in knots. Was she talking about a relationship? Sex?

Worry pulled at her. She wasn't good at relationships; they had never gone well for her family. What was she doing, thinking she could have one? That it would work at all?

But maybe Nick was different. Maybe it could work.

"Is this really the right time?" Emma murmured, only half aware she was speaking the words out loud.

"If I waited for the right time, it would never come," Nick said, solemnly. "We're always going to have things on our plates. Distractions."

Emma straightened up. Nick was right, she was acting like a teenage girl, not the woman she was. She was strong. She'd survived so much.

Surely, she could survive a relationship.

"Does it really change anything?" Nick asked, cocking her head to the side.

Emma frowned at her before she saw the teasing grin. Looking around for a pillow, she snagged one off the bed and gently hit her with it.

"Rude," Nick said, winking.

Emma rolled her eyes, but there was a crinkle in the corner of her eyelids. Warm and fuzzy feelings started in her stomach, spreading throughout her body. She had read the romance books, read all about how someone's touch on her skin could send sparks flaring and build a heat inside her.

But she'd never experienced it until now. She hadn't even thought it was possible.

"My head hurts," Emma admitted.

"We don't have to do anything." Nick gently shifted until Emma was sitting on the side of the bed.

Emma sank into the mattress gratefully, suddenly aware of how tired she was. At the same time, she didn't feel tired at all. It was that weird line between exhaustion and alertness, one she had straddled before when work demanded it.

"I want to do something," Emma said, meeting Nick's eyes.

Heat flared in Nick's eyes. Emma swallowed thickly, feeling the moisture gather between her legs at the look on Nick's face.

Nick's eyes flickered to the door, then back to Emma.

Emma frowned slightly.

"Lady Grey can be a voyeur," Nick explained.

Emma snorted, but the smile was back on her face.

Nick sat next to her, and they sat there, just looking at each other. Instead of awkward, a warm sense of peace sat in Emma's middle. Heat was pulsing through her body, her body felt on high alert, but she could have sat there and examined Nick's face for hours.

Of course, there were far more interesting things she wanted to do.

"Lay down," Emma said, nodding to the bed.

"Your head -"

"Lay down." Emma stuck her tongue out at Nick.

Nick sighed, then stood. With an air of confidence she started pulling off her top, sliding down her pants.

Part of Emma wanted to help, but there was a chunk of her that was perfectly fine with watching as every inch of Nick's body was revealed. That was one of the benefits of short-haired girls, their hair didn't hide their boobs.

Nick was lean and graceful-looking, but there were muscles there, too. She had small but perfectly sized breasts, and as she slid her pants off, her legs went on for miles.

"Here." Emma stopped her before she could take her bra off, instead gesturing for Nick to turn slightly.

Nick did, baring her back to Emma.

There was a scar on her shoulder blade, and another one on her lower left that curved across her side. Emma touched the first one with her fingers, feeling the raised bump that scar tissue left.

"Been involved in a few fights in my life," Nick said cheerfully, but it felt forced.

Emma kissed the mark. "You don't have to say anything."

Nick nodded once, and fell silent.

Part of Emma did want to know all of her stories, every single bit about her. But Emma knew how complex life got. Would she want to spill every detail of her life, especially when things were this new?

Emma unhooked Nick's bra, pulling it gently down her arms.

"Your turn," Nick said pointedly.

"I thought I told you to lay down," Emma grumbled good-naturedly, standing up.

"I don't always do what I'm told." Nick winked.

Emma rolled her eyes. She took a deep breath before pulling off her shirt, grimacing as she tried to get it over her head without hurting. She looked down doubtfully at her pants, not certain she could get them off without getting vertigo.

"Here." Nick slid off the bed, dressed in just her underwear. She undid the button of Emma's jeans, then slowly slid them down.

It was more sensual than Emma had expected. Well, it had been some time since she had had sex. Maybe that was why her senses were so heightened, and it totally wasn't tied to Nick.

Then Nick was standing, and Emma was in just her underwear.

She looked at Nick, then leaned forward, kissing her and molding their bodies together. It had been a long time since Emma had had another body against her, someone touching her.

"Can I try something?" Emma asked against Nick's lips.

Nick pulled back, studied Emma for a second and then nodded.

"Lay down." Emma's command was gentler this time.

Nick did.

Her bedcovers were light blue, like the sky, with a geometric pattern that was oddly comforting. It wasn't the first time Emma had seen the bedcovers, but it was the first time she had paid attention.

She laid down next to Nick, who was lying on her back. Emma propped her head up with a hand, surprised that it didn't hurt as much as she had expected. Maybe it supported her head and neck.

Yes, it was much easier to get caught up in the details of what was going on instead of focusing on the gorgeous woman in front of her.

She reached over and gently touched Nick's thigh furthest away from her. "Leg up."

Nick pulled her left leg up, bending it at the knee and propping her foot on the bed. Emma poked it, letting Nick's leg fall away from her body.

"This is a good way to stretch my thigh muscles," Nick muttered.

Emma grinned, shifting closer. She took her head off her hand, putting more of her weight on her forearm, but getting close enough that she could kiss Nick.

She kissed Nick, sliding her tongue into her mouth and getting lost in the heat between the two of them. It was enough to make her dizzy, light-headed, to make the thudding in her head go away, to replace it with only the two of them.

Nick moaned softly into her mouth.

Emma cupped her breast, pinched the nipple lightly, and was rewarded with Nick flinching under her. Slow and lazy. That was how she wanted it.

She stroked her hand across Nick's skin, shifted so that they were pressed together, Emma's body against Nick's side, her legs open for Emma to access.

"What can I do?" Nick's eyes opened, and she broke the kiss.

"Do the same for me?" Emma winked.

Nick chuckled, shifting slightly to slide a hand between Emma's legs, stroking her.

Emma's breath hitched, and she shifted her hips so Nick could have better access. She leaned in to kiss her, keeping the kiss slow and messy. Sliding her fingers under the waistband of Nick's underwear, she moved slowly, torturously, until she could slide a finger inside of her.

Nick's breath hitched, and Emma smiled.

Then she felt Nick's fingers on her hips, splaying across her leg. Emma's eyes fluttered closed for a second, letting out a loud moan.

Nick stopped, and Emma internally winced.

"Sorry," she said sheepishly.

"Just not what I expected." Nick grinned, then kissed her.

Emma slid a second finger inside Nick, keeping the movements slow and torturous as she started to circle her clit with her thumb. She slid her tongue against Nick's, felt Nick's fingers slide into her, and started to pump her hips slightly. Her whole body felt flushed, all of her nerve endings were on fire.

She let out a second moan, unable to hold back the hitch in her breath.

"You're gorgeous," Nick murmured.

Emma lifted her hips up towards Nick's hand in return, dying for more of her fingers inside her and the slow, sensual torture of her thumb just brushing her clit before backing off.

The crash of her orgasm hit her harder than she expected, her hips lifting as she tightened around Nick's fingers, letting out loud, breathy squeaks as the pleasure surged through her.

Thank God Nick didn't have neighbors. Or live in an apartment.

She was just starting to come down from the high when she felt Nick's hand on hers, holding her hand between Nick's thighs. It was hotter than Emma had expected.

Emma moved her hand faster, her fingers sliding in and out as she brushed against her clit, feeling each little breathy bump and movement that Nick made. It was addictive, watching her like that.

But not nearly as addictive as watching Nick's face when she came, the pleasure short-circuiting her brain, her eyes fluttering, back arching, ecstasy written all over her.

"Good?" Nick asked, her voice breathy.

Emma laid against her, her body now half on top of Nick's, letting them be close. "I guess," she said, her voice teasing. She slid an arm around Nick's waist, snuggling up next to her. "I think the painkillers kicked in." Either that or it was the endorphins. Emma was fine either way, in all honesty.

She felt Nick kiss her head. "You should sleep," Nick said, stroking her hair.

Emma looked up at her. "But what about round two?"

Nick laughed. "There's time for that in the morning."

CHAPTER NINETEEN

Monday, September 19th, 2016. 10:52pm.

Nick stroked Emma's hair down her back, delighting in the feel of Emma's warm, naked body against hers. They should have been sleeping, but it wasn't quite as simple as that. Lady Grey had returned to the room, curled up at the foot of the bed. She seemed entirely unbothered by their state of undress, which didn't surprise Nick at all.

"What are you thinking about?" Emma asked.

Nick looked down at her. "That we should be sleeping."

Emma chuckled, but it was a sleepy sound. Nick felt pleased. "Sometime," Emma agreed.

Nick fell quiet again, her mind wandering. It was the first time she had been with someone since Sarah died. The first time she had made love with someone, the first time she had been truly intimate with another person. It was a level of vulnerability that she had missed, had craved.

She hadn't expected to encounter this feeling so soon.

"How did you become the owner of Belle's House?" Nick asked, dragging her mind away from her late wife.

"I grew up there," Emma said, not looking at Nick. "My Mom and I, anyway." She inhaled slowly, Nick could feel her breathing. At the foot of the bed, Lady Grey stretched out. "I never really knew my Dad. He came around sometimes, but never for long. And when he was there, I spent most of my time hiding."

"He abused your mother?" Nick put the pieces together. Emma had mentioned that the House was named after her mother, but Nick hadn't realized the extent to which that was relevant.

"Yeah." Emma's thumb stroked Nick's side.

Nick loved laying like that, Emma's bodyweight against her and Lady Grey at the foot of the bed. It felt comfortable. It felt like home.

"He left for good when I was seven. I never saw him after that, although I think my Mom did. She never talked about him any more." Emma sighed. "She died of a broken heart when I was seventeen. I inherited the house."

Nick's heart broke. She could only imagine what

that must have been like, Emma living with a mother she loved, who in return had loved the man who hurt her.

"Abuse is complicated that way," Emma said, her voice sad. "It's too easy to love the ones that hurt us."

Nick nodded. It was something she had seen in her time as a police officer, even if it wasn't something she had experienced herself.

"I lost my wife," Nick said, sharing a part of herself with Emma. She had talked about it before, Emma had seen the photos, but Nick wanted to lay it all out.

"How did you meet her?" Emma asked.

Nick leaned down and pressed a kiss to Emma's hair. She didn't feel like she was betraying Sarah, or letting her down. Sarah would have wanted her to find someone to love. She would have wanted Nick to be happy. "She was on the force with me," she said. "Sometimes we worked the same shifts, sometimes opposite. But she had picked up an extra shift to cover the week before our anniversary." Nick swallowed thickly.

Emma hugged her gently, or as much of a hug as one could do while laying on another person.

"I didn't know anything had happened until they showed up at my door," Nick said. "When I saw my shift commander, I knew something bad had happened." Her voice cracked despite herself.

"How long ago was it?" Emma's voice was apologetic.

"About three years." Nick let out a slow breath. "She would have wanted me to move on, though. She wouldn't have wanted me to mourn her for the rest of my life."

Emma was quiet for a few moments, and Nick could see the wheels turning in her mind.

"What about you?" Nick asked, daring. "Are you dating anyone?"

Emma snorted, but she didn't look at Nick. "After growing up with my Mom the way she was, I didn't think dating was for me."

Nick could understand that. Sarah's mother had been in an abusive relationship, and that had impacted how she and Sarah had related. "What about now?"

Emma paused. "Are you asking if we're dating?"

"I dunno," Nick said. "Are we dating?"

Emma stroked her fingers against Nick's skin, seemingly distracted by the feeling. "Are we?"

"I asked you that question." Nick smiled faintly.

"We could try," Emma said doubtfully. "I don't know if I'm good at it." Guilt seemed to flash across her face. "But we need to find the killer first."

Nick leaned in to kiss her briefly. "We will. But we can't stop our lives forever."

Emma seemed doubtful, but she didn't say anything.

Lady Grey stretched further, sticking her paws into their legs.

"Half of this bed is hers," Nick said with a grin.

"Apparently," Emma said dryly. "We'll have to get a bigger bed."

Surprise flashed across both of their faces, but there was a faint happiness there, too. It was early, yes, but something had bound them together so securely that Nick doubted it would be broken.

"We should sleep," Nick said, glancing at the clock. They had to be up in less than six hours. Emma was due meds in two hours, and Nick was going to have to check on her throughout the night.

Emma made a doubtful noise.

"Here." Nick shifted slightly, reaching out to grab her phone and scroll through the screen. It was way too bright in the dim light of her room, but she wasn't going to bother to adjust the brightness only to have to fix it in the morning. She didn't want to have the TV on to aggravate Emma's head, since light could be more of a problem than noise.

She scrolled through her music, picking a playlist and turning it on. She wasn't embarrassed to admit she was fond of silly, cheesy, pop songs. She even enjoyed Katy Perry every now and again.

"I can change it if you want," Nick added, just in case Emma didn't share her fondness for pop music. She didn't know what type of music Emma liked, but it was among the many things she looked forward to finding out.

"It's fine," Emma said, and Nick could feel the smile on her face.

"Get some sleep." Nick kissed her forehead and then snuggled closer to Emma, holding her securely.

CHAPTER TWENTY

Tuesday, September 20th, 2016. 7:22am.

Nick strode into work, guilt tugging at the corner of her mind. She wasn't betraying Sarah, she knew it. Sarah would have wanted her to move on.

So why was she feeling so uneasy?

"Long time no see," Spencer drawled.

Nick rolled her eyes, and she felt some of the tension drain from her shoulders. "I see you're in a dramatic mood this morning."

"I've got updates for you." Spencer pointed to a chair next to his. Nick sank down into it, crossing her legs and settling her notebook on top of them. Her brain was scrambled, so notes would help her keep track of things until her brain was less scrambled.

"We found a diary in Conner's place," Spencer said.

Nick's eyes widened. "When?"

"Last night, around 10." Spencer kept his voice gentle. "It was overlooked in the initial search, hidden in a secret compartment underneath a desk drawer."

Nick's cheeks flushed. It had been when she was with Emma. "Sorry, I was—"

"Distracted, I know." There was kindness in Spencer's face. "I'm glad to see you've found someone."

"I haven't - we haven't…" Nick didn't know how to end that sentence, or even what to say about it. Technically they had talked about it, and sort of come to an agreement, but Nick wasn't entirely certain she wanted that to be part of anyone else's knowledge base quite yet.

"The diary was Rachel's," Spencer said, pulling an evidence bag out from his desk. "There were several entries ripped out, including ones for the week leading up to her murder."

Nick's eyebrows raised.

"Sadly, he's not our murderer."

Nick deflated. "He finally came up with an alibi?"

"Yup." Spencer sighed. "Several witnesses confirmed they saw him in a gay bar the night Rachel was killed."

Ah. That explained a lot, in Nick's opinion. She had met people like that before.

"So where are we going next?" There was Eric to look at. Ryan, too. But they didn't have any more immediate leads.

"I think we need to look more into Ryan," Spencer said.

"Why not Eric?" There had been something off about Eric. There was something off about the whole damn case, something Nick couldn't put her finger on.

"His alibi is shaky; he said he was at home sleeping with his wife at the time of Julia's murder." Spencer sounded doubtful. "But she swears he was there and the security system wasn't set off."

"How accurate is our time of death?" Nick flipped through her notebook, glancing at some of her prior notes. Julia's time of death was roughly 10pm-3am, and Rachel's was a six hour window of 6pm to midnight. That was the hard thing about real life. Time of death was hard to pinpoint.

"The usual," Spencer answered.

"What are the differences between the cases? Maybe it's not the same killer." She sounded unsure, and she felt doubtful.

"Let's include your girlfriend in the mix too," Spencer added. "Her attack may very well be related to the murders."

Nick scowled at the thought. She had checked on Emma before she left, had made sure that she had taken her meds. Then Nick had skedaddled to work as fast as she could.

"So Julia was murdered away from her home, by blunt force trauma to the head." Nick flipped through the file she grabbed off her desk, wishing she had a whiteboard to draw on.

"There was evidence of an injection, which toxicology revealed to be diazepam." Spencer was looking at a different file. "Common name is valium."

"Rachel was murdered in her home, blunt force trauma to the head. No signs of moving or the same injection. But her home was very close to Julia's." Nick was troubled. The modus operandi, or MO, were close enough that she was fairly confident that they had been committed by the same person. She didn't believe in coincidences. But could they prove it?

"Conner's alibi was airtight?" Nick looked pointedly at Spencer.

Spencer looked unhappy. "We've got video proof of him in the club, and several witness statements."

"Damn." Nick slapped the file back on the table. "Damn it, damn it, damn it!" She wanted to use several more choice words, but police detectives were supposed to be professional in public or something.

"What's the evidence that they're not connected?" Spencer asked.

"The difference in locations. Julia wasn't murdered at home, Rachel was. The injection in Julia's arm but not Rachel's." Nick recited them like she had memorized them, and she had.

"What's the evidence that they are connected?"

"Similar victim type, similar location. Both died of

blunt force trauma to the head, with some level of overkill." Nick made a thoughtful noise. "The victims knew each other, which makes the coincidence very difficult to ignore."

"Maybe Julia fought more than Rachel did?" Spencer suggested. "Perhaps that's why she was given the injection, but not Rachel."

Nick flipped through Julia's autopsy report. "That could be the case," she said. "The injection was done prior to death, which would be consistent with her maybe putting up a struggle." She grabbed Rachel's report, flipping through it. "No evidence Rachel put up a struggle." She frowned. That wasn't consistent with the woman she had met. "Could Rachel have been caught off guard?"

Spencer considered the suggestion. "She could have," he agreed.

Nick flipped through the autopsy reports, looking specifically for the trajectories of the blows. "Both were hit from behind," she said thoughtfully. "But Julia was found near the main area of the living room, with drag marks. Rachel was found in her living room, but barefoot. No drag marks."

"Maybe Julia had been trying to flee?"

"Which would mean that Julia may have known her killer?" Nick considered that, then shook her head. "It could go either way. She could have known her killer and knew he was coming to kill her, or she could have been fleeing an intruder."

"We're going in circles," Spencer said wryly.

"Welcome to detective work." Nick's voice reflected his. "Where are forensics at the moment?"

"The owner of the blood on the pants has been cleared. The girlfriend - Kylie - dropped off her dog's hair, we're comparing that to some hairs we found at Rachel's crime scene. We found a few foreign hairs at Julia's crime scene, but…" He trailed off.

"Given the high prevalence of homeless going in and out of the empty condos, it's not likely we're going to find anything." Nick grimaced.

Allison appeared in the corner of Nick's gaze, drawing her attention. "I found something on one of your suspects, a guy called Ryan Davis," she said.

"Oh?" Nick took the file she offered. It was from a different but neighboring county. "Charges?"

"He's a suspect in a few rapes in Cowlitz County. Broke into the woman's home with a baseball bat, raped her and left. Was careful to keep the condom, but he left a few pubic hairs behind." Allison gestured for Nick to flip the page.

She did, and her heart stopped. She grabbed Julia's autopsy report and flipped through it, looking for the toxicology report. Diazepam, brand name Valium.

She went back to the prescription that had been put in the file.

"Ryan has a prescription for the same drug that was found in Julia's bloodstream," Nick said grimly.

"Does he have the background to mix it?" Spencer asked, standing without preamble and grabbing his coat. No matter the answer, that put Ryan higher up on their list of suspects. Conner been cleared, Eric was still in the running, but Ryan now had the means, had a potential motive, and had a background of similar crimes.

Maybe they had hit the jackpot.

"Why didn't these show up when we ran a background check?" Nick asked, grabbing her jacket and sliding it on.

"They hadn't been entered in the system yet," Allison answered promptly. "I have a couple friends in that office, so when they heard about our case, they sent me the files."

"You're fabulous," Nick told her, and she meant it. "Let's go."

CHAPTER TWENTY-ONE

He watched from his car as the lady - Emma - and that detective left the station. Together. Alive. He frowned at the baseball bat on the floor of his car, out of sight from prying eyes. How had she survived? Had he simply not hit her hard enough?

His eyes narrowed. Oh, no. He watched as Nick the detective reached over and smoothed a lock of Emma's hair back. There was an intimacy, an affection to the gesture that he didn't like. No. No, women should marry men. Not other women.

"Stupid," he muttered to himself. That wasn't his problem.

"You have other things to focus on," Jeffrey reminded him.

He glanced back at the backseat, where Jeffrey was

sitting. "I know," he snarled. He pinched the bridge of his nose, exhaled slowly. "I have different priorities."

"What's the next step?" Jeffrey asked.

He scowled. "I don't need you to hold my hand."

Jeffrey scoffed. "You wouldn't have lasted this long without me."

He didn't want to admit it, but it was probably true.

"You left your present. Let's go home." Jeffrey was the one who spoke.

He sighed. His brother was right. Shifting the car into gear, he looked up into the rear-view mirror.

Jeffrey was gone.

CHAPTER TWENTY-TWO

Tuesday, September 20ᵗʰ, 2016. 5:27pm.

It wasn't exactly the outcome that Emma had hoped for, having Nick as a babysitter. Not that she really minded - she liked spending time with Nick - but she wanted to be out there, charging around and finding her ladies' killer.

But noooo, she'd been sent back to Belle's House with a babysitter. An attractive babysitter, but a babysitter nonetheless.

She crossed her arms, sitting in the passenger seat of Nick's cruiser. The police cruiser was higher tech than she had expected. The computer Nick could use had folded up into the visor, releasing the spot for Emma to sit.

Nick had updated her on the case, how Spencer and their unit were out looking for Ryan. Did Nick resent her, that she was stuck babysitting Emma while Spencer went and looked for the killer? Or did she not mind?

Emma didn't want to say anything, so she didn't. The last thing she wanted to do was to draw Nick's attention to it if she hadn't started resenting her yet.

Nick pulled into a spot and parked, quietly powering down the car and ensuring all the lights were off.

Emma looked at the lights on in Belle's House. The women needed to be evacuated, if they hadn't been already. Emma had been attacked, and it meant someone knew the address of their safe location. The women weren't safe there any longer.

The bastard who had attacked her was clever, picking the far side of the car and keeping his head down to avoid any ability to identify him via the security cameras. Emma had already seen the footage, and it was the security guard who had dialed 911.

She got out of the car, glancing around the parking lot out of habit. Her car was still there, so were a couple of others, but about half of them were gone. That was probably good, right?

Then there was a car parked farther away, just out of sight of the cameras. Erratically, as if the person wasn't used to parking there or the protocol.

Emma's heart started beating faster. Surely there was an innocent reason for it.

"Nick." When she caught Nick's attention, she nodded in the direction of the car.

Nick's hand went to the gun on her hip. "Get behind me."

Emma did.

"Do you recognize the car?" Nick asked, her voice soft and her eyes focused on what was in front of them.

Emma tried to focus, but it was hard to see in the dim light. "Maybe," she admitted.

Nick glanced around the forest. "Stay close to me."

Suddenly the forest seemed frightening. The shielding that had felt so protective now felt ominous, as if someone was going to jump out of it. Was the killer there? Or was it just a coincidence?

It had to be.

Leaves crunched under their feet as they walked forward, step by careful step. Although the sun hadn't fully set yet, the rays it could cast through the thick grove of trees were minimal.

Nick reached out and put an arm across Emma's chest, stopping her. They were only five or so feet away from the car.

"What?" Emma tried to peer harder, but seeing in the dark wasn't her best skill.

Then she saw it.

A pair of feet sticking out from underneath the car. Dark-covered shoes. Female tennis shoes.

A sick feeling settled in Emma's stomach, making

her head throb and her body start shaking. No. No, it couldn't be.

She heard Nick talking into her radio, heard her calling dispatch and asking for a forensics unit.

"We can't move the body," Nick said, her voice low and apologetic.

Emma barely heard her. Body? No, surely it wasn't a person. Surely it wasn't someone dead. Ignoring Nick's warnings and attempt to stop her, she circled around the car to the other side. The woman's head was mostly hidden under the car, but she could see her hair matted with blood. See the blood spatter that decorated the side of the car.

Her stomach heaved. She felt Nick's arm around her shoulders, guiding her towards the underbrush, and barely made it before the contents of her stomach emptied itself on the ground.

Her head spun, the ground almost moving around her. She was queasy, woozy, and wasn't sure if she could stand. Her doctor probably wasn't going to be very happy.

"I've got to check on the others." Emma forced herself to stand up, to shake it off. She couldn't break down, she couldn't cry. No.

Leaving Nick to handle the detective crew when they got there, Emma headed straight inside, leaving Nick behind. She had other things to focus on.

She went straight to security. "Is anyone signed

out?" If any of the women left the house, they were recorded, so they could keep track of their comings and goings and ensure everyone's safety.

The guard picked up the clipboard, her eyes skimming it. "Melanie left to get groceries about an hour ago, to prep for the evacuation. She should be back soon."

Julia's roommate. Emma was almost certain the body was hers. Was it connected? It had to be.

But how had he found them? How had he tracked her to Belle's House, killed her here? Had she actually made it to the grocery store, or had she been caught before she had left the property? How long had she been lying out there?

"What's wrong?" The security guard looked at her with a frown. Emma didn't know what to say. She was pretty certain if she looked at the security tapes, it was far away and fuzzy enough that the guard hadn't been able to see anything.

Then Vicky appeared, a frown on her face. "What's wrong?"

Emma shook her head, then gestured at Vicky to come closer. Vicky did. "There's a dead body in our parking lot," Emma said, the words feeling surreal even as they came out of her mouth.

Vicky's eyes widened, her mouth opening as if she had something to say and then closing when no words came out. "What?"

"I think it's Melanie." Emma was grim. "We need to move the ladies to other locations, ASAP."

Vicky seemed to shake the shock off, then nodded.

"Call Heart Home, Second Chances, and Angel to see if they have any spots for our ladies." They were three other vaguely local domestic violence shelters that Emma had worked with at one point or another. Even if they didn't have space, they could help her find some.

Vicky nodded, immediately disappearing out of the main room. Emma turned to the security guard.

"There's going to be a police presence in the parking area," she said. "Don't let anyone out unless escorted by staff, but some detectives may come in for questioning."

The security guard nodded, her eyes concerned.

"I'll escort them," Emma said, hoping Nick wouldn't mind. No, Nick wouldn't mind.

She wanted to find this killer as much as she did.

EMMA DIDN'T KNOW what time it was. The sun was out now. All her women had been relocated, and her head was threatening to split in two. Nick had come by a few hours earlier to confirm it was Melanie's body. Belle's House was empty. What would she do with her staff? They couldn't use it as a DV shelter, not any more, not with its location compromised.

Maybe they could start over somewhere else, somewhere new. But what would she do with the house?

No. She could think about that later. She had other, more important things to focus on.

"Hey." Nick's voice caught her off guard. She lifted her head, looking at her - whatever Nick was - with a tired smile. Or as much of a smile as she could manage, anyway.

"Everything wrapped up?" Emma asked. Nick had been working as hard as Emma had, at least from what Emma had seen. She had been busy coordinating the crime scene developments. Even Spencer had come by, talked to Nick, and then left again.

"Mostly." Nick let out a long sigh. "The crime scene techs are combing the nearby area in case they can find anything. We're going to send our specialty team to search the nearby forest later, just in case."

"Do -" Emma swallowed thickly. "Do you think she was murdered here?"

Nick's eyes flickered back to the car and where it was. "Maybe," she said. "The blood on the car indicates she was murdered near it. But whether or not this was the actual crime scene..." She looked doubtful for a moment. "It seems awfully risky."

"It had to be someone who knew how the cameras operated, and what their range was." Emma hated the words. The only people that knew that were those that were tied to Belle's House. Her co-workers. The women she helped protect.

"Or someone who knew someone here," Nick added.

Emma frowned. "What do you mean?"

Nick sighed. "We won't know until we get the autopsy report, but there's a chance that she was tortured before she was killed."

"What?" Emma was almost speechless.

"She's got some recent bruises and a break, that we could see. All predates her death." Nick grimaced. "And she hasn't been dead long, so they had to be a few days old."

"But she's been at Belle's House and fine," Emma tried to argue.

But Emma hadn't been there to check. Paranoia caused goosebumps on her arms. Could it be one of her workers? No, that was impossible. She had an entirely female staff. Surely these murders had been carried out by a man.

Right?

Oh God. Now she was just being ridiculous. There was no way it was one of her staffers.

"Hey," Nick said again, her voice soft. She drew Emma's attention in a warm way, her hand on Emma's shoulder.

It was oddly comforting, the touch, the feeling of

Nick's hand and attention on her. Emma wanted to lean into it, hug her. Could she?

She reached out and wrapped her arms around Nick, not caring who could see. Nick hesitated - Emma could feel it in her shoulders - and then wrapped her arms around Emma.

It was nice, having the warm body of someone who cared about her to provide solace in her darker days. When Nick pressed a kiss to her temple, Emma almost melted. Not out of gushy-happiness, but frustration. Sadness.

How could losing people she cared about have led to one of the better things in her life?

"If they hadn't died, I may have never met you," Emma said softly, the words leaving her mouth before she could pull them back.

"You can't change it," Nick said back.

It sounded a lot like a conversation that Nick had had with herself more than once.

"Do you think about that a lot?" Emma asked.

Nick nodded, letting go of Emma but taking her hand. "All the time," she said. "Life does what it wants. Some people call it destiny, some people call it fate. I call it luck."

"So we were lucky enough to meet?" Emma tried to crack a grin and failed.

Nick did smile. "Yes."

Emma wiped her eyes with the back of her hand,

suddenly aware of the tears falling down her cheeks. She wasn't crying, but she couldn't stop them. She was so damn tired. Her head still hurt, another one of her women had been murdered, and all she wanted to do was for the world to stop existing.

Except not really, because that would mean that Nick was gone too, and Emma didn't want that.

"Let's get you home," Nick murmured.

Emma wiped her eyes one last time, determined to stop crying. "Okay."

CHAPTER TWENTY-THREE

Wednesday, September 21ˢᵗ, 2016. 1:17am.

It should have been easy to sleep. Nick knew that. But it never was, even with Emma's warm body pressed against hers.

Emma had finally fallen asleep, exhaustion and her head injury taking a toll. She had done so much, experienced so much trauma; it worried Nick. Could Emma keep going at the rate that she was?

Lady Grey shifted at the foot of the bed, snuffling in her sleep before stretching out. Nick couldn't help a smile. She loved the cantankerous beagle, even if she was determined to kick both Nick and Emma out of her bed and steal it for her own.

Nick looked back at Emma sleeping. She could only see the back of her head, but she could feel her breathing. That was the disadvantage of being the big spoon.

You got to see part of your partner, but not always the important parts.

Partner. The word resonated in Nick's mind. Was that what Emma was? Had she gotten attached so quickly? Her mind drifted back to the night they had shared, the words they had shared. They had never officially discussed the words, or anything.

But Nick knew she would do whatever it took to help Emma find justice for the women she cared so deeply about.

Lady Grey stirred again, drawing Nick's attention. Maybe she needed water, or needed to pee. But that never stopped her from getting up on her own.

Carefully extracting herself from Emma, Nick sat up, propped on her elbows as she looked at Lady Grey with a frown.

Lady Grey's ears were perked, her nose sniffing the air and moving this way and that.

Then Nick smelled it. The faint, ashy smell of smoke.

Fire.

"Wake up." She touched Emma's shoulder, trying to be as gentle as she could in waking her in consideration of the danger. If she had to, she'd throw Emma over her shoulder, Lady Grey over the other, and carry them both out.

"What?" Emma blinked, rubbing her eyes as she sat up.

"There's smoke." Nick got out of bed, aware of being dressed in a shirt and underwear. Not the best fire-fighting attire, especially given the time of year.

"What?" Emma sounded more fully awake now. Lady Grey was standing on the edge of the bed, her bark resonating through the room.

Nick looked around for her phone, grabbing it and tucking it in her pocket. Then she reached out and felt the door. It wasn't hot. Not yet, anyway. But she could smell the acrid smell of smoke and burning wood. It wasn't safe.

"C'mon, we need to get out of here." Nick reached out and grabbed a pair of pants, sliding them on. Shoes she could deal with later. Her feet wouldn't freeze to death. Theoretically.

Emma got out of bed, looking frantically around Nick's bedroom.

"Here." Nick tossed her a pair of sweatpants. She didn't know if her jeans would fit, so they were the next best option.

The fire may not even be near them. Maybe it was coming in from the window. But Nick was getting her and Emma out of there anyway.

"Follow me." Nick turned to Lady Grey. "C'mere, girl." She scooped Lady Grey up, who was happy to lick her face. While it was normally reassuring, Nick couldn't stop her heart from beating faster.

She pushed open the door slowly at first, just in

case there was a fire out there, waiting for a burst of oxygen. Nothing happened. She could smell the smoke more strongly now, and she wished she had thought to grab something they could put over their faces. Smoke inhalation was almost more dangerous than the fire.

She leaned over the balcony, looking down at the first floor. She could see the flames flickering in the kitchen, the small tendrils reaching out and licking the walls. But the stairs were safe. Thank god.

Glancing back, she saw Emma right behind her, her face both blank and terrified. Nick could only imagine. Finding out another one of her charges had been murdered, getting hit over the head - she could only imagine what Emma was dealing with in her mind.

Turning her attention back to the stairs and the immediate problem, Nick started down to the first floor, testing each step carefully one by one. It was easier said than done, especially with a 30-pound dog in her arms, but Nick had lived there long enough that she knew the stairs without having to look at them. She could feel the smoke clogging up her lungs, feel the urge to hack whatever was gathering there up before it could harm her. Not yet. They had to get out.

"You doing okay?" Nick looked back at Emma, who was a few steps behind. That was okay. It was understandable, even.

Emma nodded, her hand on the banister and her fingers curled around it.

Nick made it down the last several steps, stopping at the bottom. She could see the kitchen now, see the flames and how they were curling towards the living room. Her whole house wasn't engulfed yet, but it was going to be.

Grabbing her phone out of her pocket, she dialed 911. The irony didn't escape her.

"Hello?" the dispatcher answered.

"I'm reporting a fire." Nick gave her address.

The dispatcher asked a few more questions that Nick barely heard over the crackling of the fire and the acrid smell of smoke threatening to suffocate her. Then someone darted past her.

"Where are you going?" Nick hissed, taking the phone away from her ear and almost dropping it. Lady Grey grumbled in protest, and Nick apologized to her.

"We have to save the case files." Emma was heading into the living room, grabbing some of the boxes and lugging them towards the door.

"Are you insane?" Nick couldn't believe her ears.

Emma turned and looked at her, determination blazing in her eyes. "We have to save the files. We have to be able to find their killer."

Nick hesitated. Most of the files were still available at the department. But all of her notes, all of her thoughts and theories on the case were in those boxes. And it was one of few places the fire hadn't reached yet. "Fine. But first I'm getting Lady Grey outside."

Emma nodded, the smoke starting to soot her face. She coughed, tears starting to stream down her face. Maybe they had been in there too long. Maybe Nick needed to abandon the files and get the hell out of there.

Nick went to the front door, grabbed the knob. Pulled.

It wouldn't open. Nick frowned, then sighed as she realized she hadn't unlocked the door. Oops.

She pulled again. It still wouldn't open.

What the hell?

"The door won't open," Nick said, panic starting to rise in her voice. The fire was getting closer and closer, the crackling terrifying and the smoke starting to obscure their vision.

"What?" Emma stood up, dropping the box next to her.

"The door won't open." Hysteria had started to sneak into her voice. Why wasn't her mind working? Surely there was a way to get out. The door wasn't the only exit.

"What's a broken window between girlfriends?" Emma's laugh was brittle, too brittle.

Nick stared at Emma, trying to comprehend her words. Then she watched as Emma ran over to the dining table, picking up one of the heavier chairs and taking aim at the window closest to the door. It was large, about waist-high. Adrenaline had let Emma lift a chair almost as big as herself.

Part of Nick felt like an idiot. Duh. Break a window, get out that way. How many times had she advised others of that? But her brain had just frozen.

Emma smashed the window, using a book to crash the rest of the glass out of the bottom frame so they could get over it safely.

"Let's go." Nick crawled over it first, ignoring the way glass bit into her legs as she crawled over it. Thank God it was a short drop onto the grass, Lady Grey in her arms. "Grab me a leash?" She pointed Emma towards Lady Grey's leash near the door.

Taking it from her, Nick clipped it to her collar and ran towards a light pole, lightly tying her leash to it. Running back to the broken window, her heart pounding, she took the boxes from Emma, both marveling and annoyed by her stubborn determination. How much was she risking? How far had the fire spread?

Nick poked her head in, daring. It was heading up the stairs now.

No, it was heading down the stairs. What? Was the fire starting in two places? Had there been a fire upstairs they hadn't seen? The smoke was puffing up into the air, destroying the air quality.

"Get out of there," Nick shouted. There was no guarantee it would stay standing, no guarantee something wouldn't collapse or roar and take Emma out.

"One more!" Emma stubbornly ran back towards the living room.

"I'm going to strangle you," Nick muttered, even though she knew she didn't mean it. She could hear faint sirens in the distance - the fire engine must almost be there.

Oh crap. The dispatcher. She'd completely forgot about her phone in the midst of everything. The call had been disconnected, although how she didn't know.

Well, she could worry about that later.

"Here." Emma thrust the box at her. Nick took it, running towards the light pole where the others were. Lady Grey was guarding them.

And by guarding, Nick meant she was sniffing and standing on them. Because why not.

At least they were sturdy boxes.

She ran back, determined to get Emma out of the damn house this time.

This time, Emma came willingly. Nick helped her get over the bits of broken glass, got her out of the house, in time for the fire engines to pull up in front of her house.

And a cop car. Crap. Spencer was never going to let her live this down.

Why the hell was she thinking about that? She had just lost her home. Her image, the teasing, was inconsequential.

Nick stood out of the way as the firefighters

emerged from their trucks, getting to work on whatever it was they needed to do to save the house. Nick normally only got involved in fires afterwards. It was rare to see one fight a fire.

"Bad night?" Spencer's voice caught her off guard. Nick was both annoyed and relieved.

"I'm guessing it wasn't an accident," Nick said grimly. She pulled Emma closer to her, aware of the sheer exhaustion in her girlfriend's body. The only thing keeping her going at the moment was the inability to give up. She had time for grief later.

"We'll know more when it's out," Spencer said, but there was an undercurrent in his cheerfulness. He was scared, and he was angry. He turned his eyes pointedly to the boxes of case files. "And what are these?"

"The case files." Emma was the one that answered.

"They have all my thoughts in them," Nick explained, sticking up for her, no matter how flat her voice was.

"You do know we have copies of these in the department?" Spencer said darkly.

"Yes, but not my stuff." Nick was stubborn.

Spencer seemed to drop the subject. There were bigger fish to fry, and Nick knew that.

"You're coming with me to the department," he said, looking between the two of them.

"What?" Emma frowned slightly, but Nick wasn't entirely surprised.

"It's for our safety," Nick said, trying to keep her voice steady. "They think this is related to the murder cases we're investigating."

Emma's eyes widened. "What?" Then her face clouded.

"It'd be an awful big coincidence for Nick to be targeted for arson randomly, after your attack." Spencer's eyes were scanning their surroundings, as if he was only half aware of them standing in front of him. Probably a remnant of his army days, if Nick had to bet. "And your front door was nailed shut."

Nick was speechless. Emma didn't speak either.

"Let's go." Spencer's voice was compassionate, and he gestured them towards the cruiser.

CHAPTER TWENTY-FOUR

There was something delightful about watching them escape the fire, even though they were still alive. They were fighters. Especially the dark-haired one. The pretty one.

Emma, that was her name. He could feel goose-bumps prickling up and down his arms. Feel Jeffrey's voice in his mind.

Do it.

Take her.

It wouldn't have been the first time he had listened to Jeffrey. Maybe he should. Besides, it couldn't be that hard, right? He'd almost caught her a few times.

With her, he wouldn't need any other women. None of those fakers who claimed to love him. No, Emma would complete him. She'd provide everything that no one else had ever given him. Julia. Rachel. Melanie. People who had tried to please him and failed.

No, Emma wouldn't join that list. She would marry him.

Or die.

CHAPTER TWENTY-FIVE

Wednesday, September 21st, 2016. 4:33pm.

"Any luck finding Ryan?" Emma looked between Nick and Spencer. She had been at the police station for hours, and was stuck there for God knows how much longer. All she wanted to do was get out there and try to find whoever was targeting her ladies.

Who had been targeting her or Nick.

"No." Spencer grimaced. "His house was empty. We're tracking other addresses for him or his family, trying to find them, but that takes time."

Nick swore and tapped her fingers on the desk.

It grated on her, Emma could tell. Part of her felt a bit guilty - Nick wouldn't have been in that spot if it hadn't been for her - but the rest of her didn't. No, come hell or high water, she was going to find what had happened to her women.

"You should probably get some sleep," Spencer said while he looked at Nick. But Emma knew he was talking to both of them.

"Take the far cot," Nick advised as she stood up.

"No." The words exploded out of Emma's mouth. "I don't want to be here. I want to go find the damn bastard that murdered my friends."

Nick looked at her, startled. Spencer's eyebrows were raised, with a wry grin on his face.

Emma's cheeks flushed. She hadn't meant to lash out. "Sorry."

"You feel helpless." Nick's voice was sad.

Emma exhaled. "Yeah." She had never felt more helpless in her life, even when her mother had been with her father. Then, she could do something about it. Here? She was stuck with her hands tied.

"Can I at least go to Belle's House?" Emma asked, trying to find some middle ground.

Nick and Spencer looked at each other. Doubt was written all over their faces.

"Please." Emma wasn't going to beg, but she was getting close.

"How about we send a patrol officer with you to get what you want from there, then bring you back to the station?" It was Nick who suggested that.

Emma almost melted from relief. She'd get out of the station, get to do some more searching. "I want to dig through the files, and see if I can find anything."

Nick nodded. "I'll get Allison to go with you."

"Thank you." Emma looked between her and Spencer, gratefulness oozing from her pores. She would have gone crazy if she had been stuck there for the rest of the day, alone with her thoughts. Hearing about the action and doing nothing to assist.

EMMA GOT out of the car, and Allison turned off the lights. It was more eerie than it had been, even on the night she had gotten hurt. The last of the sun's rays spread out through the forest, casting golden beams across the floor.

Taking her keys out of her pocket, she headed towards the front door. The lot was empty.

"Is anyone here?" Allison asked.

Emma shook her head. "I doubt it," she answered. "With the ladies gone, we'd only keep a skeleton crew here. And I sent them home."

Allison nodded, apparently considering this. "What if -"

"What if something happens here?" Emma's lips twisted. "I don't know." She could rebuild, if it was lit on fire. Or if something else happened to it. But she didn't know what was going to happen.

She opened the front door. It was a long time since

Belle's House had been so quiet, and it got under her skin. Reminded her too much of the past.

Part of her wished that Nick was there with her. For what, Emma didn't know. Her comfort, maybe? But Nick had her own job to do, and Emma could deal with anything if it meant finding out who killed her ladies.

Her phone rang. Tucking it to her ear, she pointed Allison towards the living room. "Go check and see if anything looks out of place in there." "Hello?" This was directed towards her phone.

"It's Nick."

Nick's voice sent relief flooding through her. Even without the whole girlfriends thing, Emma would have been relieved. But that added an extra dimension. "Hey." Emma's voice was softer than she would have expected. "What's up?" Was Nick just calling to check on her, or was there another reason?

"Found a booby trap at Ryan's backup location, set to explode," Nick said, her voice weary.

Emma's blood ran cold. "What?"

"We caught it before anyone went inside," Nick said. "But it was close."

"What does that mean?" Emma clutched the phone tighter to her ear, as if that would help.

"Well, he's definitely our prime suspect at the moment." Nick was grim. "We've got a BOLO out to all the neighboring counties. We think he may have one more place, but we can't find it."

Emma rocked back on her heels. She started moving, heading towards the therapy offices. Maybe she could find something that could help the case. "Is there anything I can do?"

"Not really." Nick paused. "Finish up looking at Belle's House, and get back to the station. He could be anywhere, Emma."

Emma swallowed thickly. There was no way he'd be here. That'd be a way too stereotypical movie. Or book. "I will. I'll call you when I'm done."

"Thanks." The call hung between them for a few moments. "Take care," Nick said.

Emma smiled. She wasn't ready to say it, either, even though she would have bet that was what she felt. "You too." She hung up, tucking her cellphone back in her pocket.

She was standing in front of the main therapy office, where all of her notes were stored. She ignored a prickle of fear that swept across her skin. It was way too cliché for him to be here. It wasn't even realistic.

Then why was she hesitating about opening the door?

She forced herself to laugh, even though it sounded hollow and bitter. Then she pushed the door open, and held her breath. Flicked on the lights.

No one was there. She let out another laugh, this one more relieved. She had built up the image in her mind, that stereotypical horror movie where the slasher was hiding in the dark room.

Still, it was creepily quiet. "Let's see, where are my notes?"

Now she was talking to herself. It kind of made sense. She had done it when she was younger - if it was quiet, she would talk to herself so that the house wasn't as scary.

The memory made her smile, half from sadness. Mom would always read her a story when she went to bed, no matter how bad her day had been or if she had bruises on her face.

Emma lifted her head slightly. That was another thing she wanted to do: search Melanie and Julia's room. It hadn't been cleared out, since Melanie still lived there. Maybe there was something in there she could use to help the case.

She left the therapy room, locking the door behind her, and headed towards Melanie's room down one set of stairs and down the hall. She hadn't been given a new roommate following Julia's departure. She never would.

Emma locked the sadness away, pushing open the door and flicking on the light. Melanie's bed was made, her clothes hanging neatly in the wardrobe that the ladies shared. It was harder than Emma had thought it would be to be objective, to think about it in terms of investigation rather than going through someone's belongings.

The police had already gone through her room, given it a detailed search, but hadn't found anything of note. The crime scene technicians had been far more interested in the crime scene outside, anyway. Maybe Emma, with her knowledge of the rooms and their history, could find something they missed.

You know, just like the movies. Emma smiled wryly. She took a deep breath and stepped forward. Where to start?

Remembering where she'd found Julia's diary, she started with Melanie's bed. She felt almost sick at the invasion of privacy, but she had to do what she had to do.

There was nothing under the covers, so she worked on pulling the mattress off its frame so she could flip it over. The mattresses were set in frames next to the wall, which made it more difficult than she had expected.

"Damnit," she swore, finally able to get the mattress off its frame and flipped. But there was nothing. She scowled at the mattress and its frame, as if that would do anything productive besides making her feel better.

She settled it back on the frame, brushing the

covers back into place as if that would do anything. But it did make her feel better. Even if Melanie wasn't coming back, Emma would make it a place that honored her.

She went to the wardrobe next. Each woman shared one with her roommate. Half of the hanging space, and two of the four drawers. She started with the hanging clothes, feeling her way through each shirt and set of pants. She checked the pockets, just in case.

Nothing.

The drawers were next. She started with the first, gently going through her intimates. The drawer seemed oddly shallow.

God, Emma had seen too many detective shows. Not that it stopped her from gently rapping her knuckles on the bottom of the drawer, or feeling underneath it from the bottom. There was a small mark, one that Emma caught with her fingertip.

She pressed it, and then jumped back when the bottom of the drawer fell out and letters swam all over the place. But the intimates stayed where they were.

Emma scowled at the drawer as if it had been hiding the secret on purpose. Then she started gathering the envelopes. What was taking Allison so long downstairs? She'd go check on her in a sec.

How had the police missed the letters? Had they been distracted by the Ryan situation? Chasing a potential murderer was probably a higher priority than searching a victim's room, especially if the murder hadn't happened there.

She sat the pile of envelopes and letters on Melanie's bed, and started pulling out the letters within. Most were from or to Julia, the other party addressed to "B". Emma frowned, skimming them as she went through them. They were love letters.

Had she ever mentioned a B in therapy?

She checked the dates on the letters. Most were prior to her moving out to the halfway house. Had Melanie kept them for her to avoid them being discovered? Or had Melanie kept them for some other reason?

Did it have anything to do with the case? None of their suspects had names that started with a B. She tapped her fingers on her thigh, thinking. Then she stuck the letters in a bundle, grabbing a hair tie off Melanie's nightstand to bundle them up. No matter what she could glean from them, she needed to get them to Nick and see if there was anything they could find in the letters that would help the case.

She wanted to check her notes, the records of her sessions with Melanie and Julia. Maybe there would be something in there.

"Hello?" Allison's voice startled her to the point she almost jumped and dropped the letters. "Sorry."

"Did you find anything?" Emma asked, straightening up.

Allison shook her head. "It's empty, and it looks like people left in a hurry."

That made sense.

"Did you find anything?" Allison looked at her, curious.

"Do you have any evidence bags on you?" Emma held out the letters.

"Of course." Allison pulled some out of her pocket, both small and gallon-sized. She scribbled on one with a pen, then held it open for Emma to drop in the letters.

"Sorry," Emma said.

"For what?" Allison blinked.

"Not wearing gloves."

Allison shrugged. "We'll take your prints and eliminate them. Can't change what already happened. Just try not to touch anything else."

"It's my house," Emma said wryly. "My fingerprints are on everything."

Allison smiled faintly. "True."

Emma led her towards her therapy room. "Is there anything else you want to look at?"

Allison shook her head. "I'll wait for you at the front door."

"I'll finish up here," Emma said. Allison nodded,

then headed out of the room without a backwards glance.

Emma put her hands on her hips, gazing back and forth across the room as she tried to figure out what she was going to start with. Her computer. That had most of her records, and then she could check the session notes she took by hand.

Logging in, she waited the few seconds for it to boot up. She had upgraded most of the computers last year, and it had paid off in terms of speed. Then she logged into the therapy system, heading straight for Julia's profile.

She found her initial records, her intake session. Emma skimmed it. No mention of who she was there to avoid. No restraining order filed. She had done everything else asked of her - attended therapy, worked on getting a new job, rebuilding her life. But she had refused to talk about the man who had hurt her.

And it was a man, they knew that much.

She started skimming the session notes, watching Julia's progress. In the beginning she had been reluctant to talk, distant and afraid. By the time Julia had been ready to move to the halfway house, she had blossomed. But she still didn't talk much about him.

Emma went to the last few sessions of the notes she had kept. Then her heart started racing.

Mentioned that he liked to rape her, that it was related to something he had seen at work. Potentially law enforcement?

Nick had mentioned that Ryan was under investigation for a rape case. Could it be...?

She grabbed her phone and dialed Nick's number. It rang, and rang.

No answer.

Emma raced downstairs to find Allison. She had to get back to the station, and fast.

CHAPTER TWENTY-SIX

Wednesday, September 21ˢᵗ, 2016. 5:37pm.

"I'll meet you at the address," Nick shouted to Spencer as he peeled out of the parking lot and she headed towards her cruiser. They had a potential address for Ryan, someone who had seen him in the vicinity. Nick had been the last one to know, the last one to head out. Spencer had been reluctant to give her the information for fear of her safety.

It was a fight to keep going, but it was all she had. Yes, she could cry over the loss of her belongings, of all the photos of her and Sarah, part of the life they had built together. But Nick didn't have time to cry, or grieve, not with a killer on the loose. All she could do was just grit her teeth and keep moving forward.

But it haunted her, that image of her house in flames. It had been the first home she had bought on her own, and it had taken her almost a year after Sarah's death to take that step.

She swallowed thickly, shoving the emotions back. She would get through it. She would move forward, like she always did. She wouldn't let the grief swallow her whole.

Her phone rang, drawing her attention. She stopped, looking at the screen. It was Emma.

Drawing her keys out of her pocket, she went to answer the phone with her other hand.

She felt the hard impact of something over her head, watched the world spin.

Then it went dark.

It wouldn't do to drive a police car when it wasn't his, no. But he was satisfied with his plan. His bait.

He nestled Nick in the trunk of his car, then patted her down. Her gun, her taser, handcuffs – he took anything and everything a cop could carry that could interfere with his plan. He had a purpose for her. She was a consolation prize that would get him what he truly wanted.

Emma.

He had watched the two of them, seen the tenderness and the affection. If he had Nick, Emma would come running.

Putting Nick's belongings on the passenger seat, he started the car and idled nonchalantly out of the parking lot. It was empty except for her cruiser and car - the other detectives had already left or were off. He had been watching for this moment, planning.

Where was he going to take her? That was simple. He was going to take her to where everything had begun.

"You're making the right decision," Jeffrey said from the backseat.

He looked up into the mirror, a smile on his face. "I know."

CHAPTER TWENTY-SEVEN

The drive back to the station felt like it took years. Nick still wasn't answering, which was unusual for her. Even though Allison didn't seem concerned, Emma was.

"Here, try Spencer." Allison passed her a small piece of paper with a number on it. Emma dialed the number, double and triple-checking it before she hit call.

It rang a few times. "Hello?" Spencer's voice sounded on the other line.

Emma let out her breath in relief. Surely Nick was with her partner, and just wasn't paying attention to her phone. That was the most logical explanation. "It's Emma. Is Nick with you?"

"She was supposed to be, but she's not here yet."

Emma wasn't sure whether the fact he wasn't

worried was reassuring or not. "I found some stuff at Belle's House that might help you with the case."

"She might be at the station," Spencer said, but Emma could hear a thread of doubt seep into his voice. "You tried her phone?"

"Twice." Emma tapped her fingers against her thigh, trying to figure out what to do.

"Head to the station, I'll meet you there." The line went dead.

Emma tucked her phone back into her pocket. "We're meeting Spencer at the station."

The car lurched forward as if it felt the driver's uncertainty, and not just because Allison had put her foot down harder on the pedals.

Emma's mind was spinning. What had happened to her? Was she just running late? Had someone caught her at the station, needed to ask a question? Maybe her phone was just dead.

It was one problem with a million solutions.

They were first to the station, with Emma opening her door and getting out before Allison even turned off the car. She searched the parking lot, trying to find any clue of where Nick had gone.

Then she saw Nick's car, and headed in that direction. It was parked in the farther-back bit of the detectives' lot, and there was a patrol car not too far away. Was it Nick's, or was it a coincidence?

She heard the sound of another car screeching into

the lot. Straightening up, she turned towards the source of the sound, suddenly aware of how defense-less she was. She'd had some training, yes, but that was useless against guns or anything long-range.

Like a car.

But it was just Spencer's patrol car. He got out, Allison heading towards him with Emma not far behind.

Emma looked between the two of them. "What?"

"We had someone check the station," Spencer started. His eyes flicked to the car behind Emma. "And that's her cruiser."

"What?" Emma repeated herself, stumbling over the words.

"She's missing," Spencer said. "No one can find her."

Emma almost sank down to her knees, but she forced herself to keep standing. "Maybe she went somewhere."

Spencer gestured for them to follow him, and Emma did, even though she felt like she was in a daze. They made it to the other side of Nick's cruiser.

On the floor was her phone. And her keys.

"She didn't leave voluntarily," Spencer said grimly.

Emma stared at the items, her eyes wide and her courage dampened. What had happened to Nick?

"Where is she?" Emma whispered, afraid of another loss after everything that had happened. Was Nick the next victim?

"We'll find her," Spencer promised.

"I want to help." Emma turned to look at him, her eyes like fire. She had already lost three of her ladies, she wasn't going to lose anyone else, especially someone who meant so much to her.

"Follow me." Spencer turned and headed towards the station.

Emma followed right behind him.

NICK'S HEAD WAS THROBBING. *Thud, thud, thud.* The fact it was not-so-gently hitting carpet every few seconds wasn't helping.

She opened her eyes, blinked. Closed them again for a few seconds and then opened them again. She wasn't blind, she was just in a trunk. Fabulous. What was more cliché than a detective being kidnapped and shoved in a stupid trunk?

She was going to have to have a stern talking-to with whoever had put her in there.

First she tested her feet. Bound, but not too tightly. She could wiggle a bit. Her wrists, however, were bound tightly. Probably cutting off her circulation. Worst case her hands would fall off.

She let out a mirthless snort. Yes, gallows humor was so appropriate at times like this.

Letting out a grunt, Nick flipped herself until she

could feel the carpet underneath her. It was just enough room to move, so probably a two or four-door sedan.

She forced herself to take a deep breath, to set the gallows humor aside for a few moments. She had to focus on getting out of there, and doing whatever she could to save herself.

Emma. She closed her eyes, forcing back thoughts of her girlfriend, or whatever Emma was. Emma was yet another reason she had to get out of there. Emma had already lost so many people, she didn't want to add herself to that list.

And Nick had already lost Sarah. The last thing she wanted to do was lose Emma when they were so close to building something together.

Nick could feel when the car started decelerating. Gritting her teeth, she tried to arrange herself so that her feet were closest to where the trunk opened. With her hands bound behind her back, she wasn't really going to be able to do much with those, but she could still kick.

The car started slowing down, oddly gentle for the rough way it had been stomping over the bumps in the road. She heard the door open, heard it close.

Should she lash out? Should she pretend to be unconscious? The thudding in her head made it hard to think.

She went limp, waiting for the trunk to open. She

had to at least make sure the person was in her direct line of action before she lashed out. It was her last chance.

The trunk popped open, letting a faint line of light in. She didn't move. Better the person think she was unconscious versus aware before she came out fighting.

"I know it's not the one I want, but I'm going to use her as bait." The voice caught her off guard. She knew that voice. It was Eric. The ADA. But who was he talking to?

He let out a frustrated noise. "I *know*, Jeffrey. Geez." The trunk got pushed up.

Nick immediately loosened her muscles. It was hard, especially when Eric reached inside and checked her bindings. But the trunk was all the way up, and that was the important bit.

She could hear Eric move, hear him shift. She tensed her thigh muscles, and lashed out.

"Son of a bitch!" Eric howled, and Nick knew her feet had connected with something. Hopefully his face, but that depended on a whole lot of timing and luck.

Latching her feet over the edge of the trunk, she tried to lever herself far enough forward that she could get out. It was harder than she had expected with her hands bound so tightly, but the Police Academy had taught her a lot. Even though they hadn't exactly counted on 'when you're bound and stuffed in a trunk, here's what you do' being something that many encountered.

The edge of the trunk scraped through her slacks, and it was one of several times that Nick had gotten frustrated that the damn fancy things were so thin. Yet, she was able to get her feet over the edge, wiggling side to side to try and get some traction forward.

Then she felt hands grasp her legs and pull her out of the trunk, letting her head hit the ground with a painful smack.

At least it was grass, Nick's dazed mind decided. She would avoid a concussion. But a sore head was only something she'd have to worry about if she survived what was going on.

Then he leaned down and checked her bindings, tightening the ones on her hands and feet even further. Her fingers were starting to tingle.

"Can you let my hands out a bit?" Nick asked, trying to keep her voice respectful. "They're cutting off the blood flow."

Eric paused in whatever it was he was doing, and Nick could see out of the corner of her eyes that he was looking up at someone. Was there a second person? They hadn't found any evidence of a second person being at the crime scenes, but that didn't mean there wasn't one.

Then he tugged on her hands, wrenching the bindings into her wrists further. Nick couldn't help but let out a yelp, the pain distracting her from what was going on in her head.

While she didn't normally hate lawyers, she could make an exception for this one.

"You could let me go," she said, helpless as he reached down and pulled her up. For a skinny, gangly man he was surprisingly strong.

He laughed, she could both hear and feel it, then his head moved as if he was sharing a laugh with someone else. But there was no one she could see or hear. "Like that would work."

Nick conceded the point. It was a useless argument with an attorney, especially one who worked regularly on criminal cases. He already knew how much trouble he was in. There was no way she could feed him the BS about how he could get a plea deal, or anything like that.

She hated smart criminals.

"I think here's a good place," Eric said, and Nick doubted he was talking to her. It was a strange sort of conversation to have, anyway. Then he shook his head, placing Nick on her feet and holding her by her bound wrists. "Forward."

Nick kept her eyes down at first, trying to make sure she wasn't going to trip on anything. They were in a forested area, a well-traveled one. That didn't make sense - wouldn't it be more sensible to take her to a less-traveled area, where they were less likely to be found?

Unless Eric wanted to be found. His words, *I know it's not the one I want*, drifted through her mind. Was Nick not his main target? Was he after someone else?

Nick's mind was working on overdrive. Was he after Emma? That would have been the person that made the most sense. Spencer would have been the other one. Maybe it was one of the other officers. Maybe it wasn't even a real person, given that Eric seemed to be talking to himself.

Then Belle's House came into view and Nick's heart skipped a beat. Why were they there? "Where are we?" she asked, even though she knew the answer.

Eric didn't answer.

"Why did you grab me?" Nick tried to keep her voice as non-confrontational as possible, trying to get him to reply.

He just grunted, pushing her forward.

Maybe there was someone in the house that could help her, save her, from whatever was going on. But after Melanie's body was discovered there, everyone had left, so she doubted it.

"Did you kill Julia?" Nick asked, daring.

That got his attention. He stopped, reaching down into whatever he was carrying with him and pulling something from the bag. It was a dirty piece of cloth.

Well, it wasn't like Nick regretted her question. She

gritted her teeth as he wrapped the gag around her mouth, trying to force it between her teeth. He tied it behind her head, then pushed her forward.

She could probably speak, even if it was muffled, but she didn't want to push him. Not until she knew more about what was going on.

THEY SAT around the briefing table, with Spencer at the head, and Emma with Allison to the left and two officers Emma only barely recognized to the right. "So Nick was last seen by the security cameras at 5:30," Spencer said, pointing to a location on a map.

"Was there anyone else on the tape?" Allison asked, her gaze flickering between Emma and the images and map in front of them.

Spencer grimaced. "If he was smart, and he probably was, you won't see him or his car. But I have people checking."

Emma sat in her chair, listening to the talking going on around her. Nick was missing. Nick had been taken. The words went on in a circle in her brain, tumbling like dice.

"Did you check her home?" Allison asked.

"The one that was burnt to the ground?" Spencer said wryly.

"Lady Grey is with friends," Emma said, trying to be helpful. "Maybe she went there to check on her."

"I'll have someone get in touch with Jordan or Carys," Spencer said, scribbling down a note. "It's something worth pursuing, anyway. What did you find at Belle's House?"

Emma looked at Allison, who produced the evidence bags. "They're letters that Julia wrote to someone named B, that I found in Melanie's room." She looked at Spencer for permission, and he nodded. She slid on a pair of latex gloves before opening the evidence bags and pulling the letters out. "I also found some evidence in the notes on my computer, which is still at Belle's House, that Julia's former boyfriend was involved in a rape case."

Spencer's eyebrows lifted. "As the defendant, or...?"

Emma shook her head. "I don't know," she admitted. "It could be either."

Spencer tapped his fingers on the table as he thought. "Ryan is the suspect in a few rape cases."

Something sparked in Emma's mind. "What about Eric? He's a prosecutor, right?"

Spencer looked at her, thoughtful. "Yes, he is." He turned to Allison. "Do you have those records? Both completed and past cases."

"And if he worked anywhere else before coming here," Emma added. Spencer looked at her. "Because the rape case was in a different jurisdiction." She shrugged, not embarrassed. If she was wrong, she was wrong. If she was right, they needed to know.

"Right away." Allison nodded, shifting her attention to the computer in the briefing room.

Emma watched her fingers fly across the keyboard, and no one spoke as Allison pulled up the database. Would that provide the lead? Who had Nick? Was there any way that she was just somewhere else?

Allison's face went ashen, drawing everyone's attention. "Eric was the prosecutor in charge of Ryan's case originally, before he transferred to Clark."

The room was silent.

"Well, shit." Spencer ran a hand through his salt-and-pepper hair before he stepped to his feet. "Call his office, see if anyone knows where he is."

"What about Ryan?" Emma asked. Was he still important?

"We need to find both of them. They could be working together." Spencer thought, his gaze far away. "Allison, get Menner's crew on Ryan's location, and my crew will start looking for Eric."

Someone popped their head in the door. "Forensics confirmed a match between the dog hairs dropped off by the victim's girlfriend and some foreign hairs in Eric's car."

"Okay maybe we need to prioritize Eric after all," Emma muttered under her breath.

Either way, she didn't care. She just wanted to find Nick.

"Is Eric the B in Julia's letters?" Spencer looked intently at her, even as the room erupted into chaos.

Emma drummed her fingers on the table, thinking hard back to her sessions with Julia. The ones she had read the notes for relating to Melanie. Could he be? "I don't know," Emma said.

"He's got a brother." Allison startled everyone. "Name's Jeffrey."

"Well, there we go." Spencer sounded relieved. Then he paused. "Are we looking for the brother or Eric?"

"Both?" Emma suggested.

"Brother is missing." Allison was clicking and scrolling through pages. "Co-workers reported him after he missed three straight days of work, saying he wouldn't do that."

"When was he reported missing?" Spencer asked.

Allison looked him dead in the eye. "The day after Julia was killed."

Emma's heart constricted. No matter who it was, Nick was still in trouble and they didn't know where to find her. "Then where is she?"

The question echoed around the table. No one knew.

CHAPTER TWENTY-EIGHT

Wednesday, September 21^{st,} 2016. 8:01pm.

Nick sat in the basement or wherever it was she had been dumped. She was blindfolded now too, accompanied just by her thoughts and the incoherent ramblings of the man who had kidnapped her.

Would she see Emma again? Would she see daylight again, her dog, her friends? She regretted not talking to Emma more. Not making things more official. She had never expected to have deathbed regrets, but there she was. It was strange what type of thoughts ran through someone's mind when they were facing potential death.

"Why did you take me?" When he had put the blindfold on her, he had removed the gag. She hadn't said anything, so he hadn't put it back on.

"Bait," Eric said absently. She could hear him shuffling around, maybe picking at something.

Was he the last thing Julia had seen?

"And revenge," he added after a few moments. He sounded oddly thoughtful, like that was the secondary motivation behind anything else he was doing.

Nick thought back to some of her Police Academy classes. The main reasons people murdered were love, money and power. "You loved her, didn't you?" Nick asked.

She could hear Eric's movements stop. "What?"

"Julia." Nick tried to keep her voice as nonjudgmental as possible, trying to prevent him from closing up or attacking her again. "You loved her."

Eric let out a long sigh. "Yes." Nick could almost hear a scowl in the tone of his voice. "But the bitch betrayed me."

"How?" Nick knew she was taking a risk with that question, but she had to know. The more information she could get, the more likely she was to get out of there alive.

She hoped.

"Doesn't matter." There was the sound of a rock hitting a wall, like he was throwing something out of boredom. "She better show up."

Nick didn't say anything to that because she didn't know what to say.

Then he let out a growl. "I fucking know. Just shut

up, Jeffrey."

But the room was silent, except for him.

Well that wasn't creepy or anything. Was he hallucinating? Or was there someone there texting him, or talking to him in another way? Maybe they were using sign language. It was hard to tell when you were blindfolded.

"Why did you kill the others?" Nick asked, her voice as casual as she could make it.

"Why do you want to know?" He sounded mulish.

Nick let out a snort. It wasn't as forced as she wanted it to be. There was too much truth in what she was going to say. "We both know the chances of me getting out of this alive aren't very high."

Eric seemed to consider this, as he let out a faint chuckle. "A realist. Too bad you're not the one I want."

Yup, Nick thought. *That's me, the realist.* It sometimes happened when you lost the person you loved most in the world. Then, when you met someone you loved, life had to put you in a situation where you were going to lose them, too.

Love made people do stupid things.

EMMA STOOD JUST outside Spencer's police car, her arms crossed as she shivered. It was colder than she had expected, and all of her coats were at home.

And Nick wasn't there to offer hers.

Emma forced the thought back, the tears back. No, it wasn't time for that. They were there executing a search warrant at Eric's address, and another team was at the brother's. Maybe they would find Nick there.

"Why am I here again?" Emma muttered to Allison, rubbing her hands on her arms to try and build some heat through friction.

"Because it's not safe to leave you behind," Allison answered, her attention on Spencer at the door. "Here we can keep an eye on you."

At least they weren't treating her like a toddler. Too much.

She glanced down at her phone, just in case a message or a call came in from Nick. A "ha-ha, just kidding!" An end to the nightmare.

But there was nothing on the screen.

She hated feeling helpless, and her life at the moment was the epitome of helplessness. She couldn't do anything. She was stuck watching, her hands kept to herself. Unable to search for the woman she loved.

Yes, love. She hated the word, but it was appropriate.

The sound of the door crashing open startled her out of her thoughts. She looked up, seeing the door splinter as the police rushed in. Yet she and Allison just stood there, eyes on the door.

It was boring. It was dreadfully useless.

"Please." She looked at Allison, who looked at her. Who knew what she was asking.

Allison sighed. "Let them clear the building, first."

A thrill of victory curled through Emma's stomach, quickly replaced by dread that they might find Nick or her body. Could she handle that? Was Allison protecting her, in case that was what they found? She dreaded the thought, dreaded someone coming out with the expression she had seen on other people's faces.

Time seemed to pass impossibly slowly before Spencer came out of the house and flashed an "all clear" sign to Allison. Then he looked at her, then Emma. "C'mon." He beckoned them close.

Allison's smile was wry. Emma darted ahead of her, beating her to Spencer.

"I figured you'd want to look," Spencer said, his eyes warm.

Emma nodded, not trusting her voice to crack or tears to leak out of her eyes when she thought about all that was at stake. He gestured her forward and she went.

The house was as creepy inside as it was outside. The staircase looked old, paint peeling. Even the furniture seemed like it was from another time. "Is the house old?" Emma asked, her brows furrowed.

"That's the interesting thing," Allison said. "From

public records, we can see it was only built ten or fifteen years ago."

"So not nearly as old as it suggests." Emma hummed thoughtfully, her attention focused solely on the place around them. It was a useful distraction. Then she emerged into the living room.

Her eyes widened. It looked almost like a funeral parlor, with flowers and photos everywhere, with pews instead of seats. "What the …?" She looked at Spencer and Allison.

"I have no idea," Spencer said wryly. "It's the first time I've seen that in a residential home, that's for sure."

"Did he have family?" Emma frowned slightly.

"Wife and son, but neither are here. No cars, no anything. It's like they disappeared." Spencer didn't sound pleased.

Emma walked forward, searching the area. There were three rows of pews, a foot or two of space between them. It was oddly reminiscent of a church, an old one that was from the 1800s. But it was a residential home. The spiral staircase went upstairs, made out of creaky wood and thin metal.

She turned her attention to the photos on the walls. They looked like genuine photographs, but those taken years ago. "There's no chance he's a ghost or anything, right?"

She wasn't sure if she was joking.

"Not that we're aware of," Spencer said, the corner of his lips threatening to curve up.

"That's reassuring," Emma said.

Everyone chuckled.

She got closer to the photos, reached out to touch one.

"Here." Allison caught her attention, passing her a pair of latex gloves.

Emma slid them on, nodding her thanks. She studied the row of photos, how they were all perfectly aligned except for three of them. With eight photos total, it was just under half.

And they were alternating.

Was it seriously going to be like the movies where there was some sort of magic that opened a secret door?

Not able to fight the curiosity, she reached for the painting that should be crooked and gently tilted it to match the others.

Nothing happened. She grinned sheepishly.

Just when she had stepped back, adjusted the painting back to where it was, a bookcase swung open.

Emma's eyebrows raised. "Wasn't expecting that."

"Neither were we." Spencer looked at it with narrowed eyes. "Stay behind us." He gestured for Allison to come forward with him, their guns in their hands.

While Emma neither used nor wanted to use a gun,

she was quite grateful for their existence at that particular moment.

Step by step they went down the set of stairs, the silence even creepier than the rest of the house.

"Holy shit." Spencer's voice echoed in the room.

Emma's heart quickened, and she wanted to push through them to get down there. But she didn't. "What?"

"You've got to see this." That was Allison, her voice as in awe as Spencer's was.

Emma's stomach was starting to twist itself into knots. What was she about to see?

She took the last few steps down the staircase, and then froze. Candles decorated the wall, the dim light casting shadows onto the wall.

The wall that was covered in photos.

There was Julia, there was Melanie. There was Eric and another man they didn't recognize. Jeffrey, maybe? Photos of Rachel's body were on the far side, with one or two obviously taken as he was sneaking up on her. The photos were dark and gritty, unlike Julia's or Melanie's. Was Rachel worth less?

There was even a photo of Emma, tucked into the corner. It was her giving Julia the keys to her condo when she finally moved out.

"Well, I guess that answers one question," Spencer said quietly.

"Does this seriously happen?" Emma looked at

Spencer and Allison. "I thought this only happened on TV."

"Every once in a while," Spencer managed to say with a straight face.

Emma snorted, surprised at how much it lightened the moment even in the bad situation.

Then a ringing sound echoed throughout the room.

The hairs on the back of Emma's neck stood up. "Whose phone is that?"

Spencer checked his phone, and a chorus of "not me" echoed around the room.

Emma's heart was racing now, goosebumps on her skin. "Is there a phone in here?" She turned slowly, looking.

"There." Spencer pointed to one of the bookcases in the corner. Tucked on the side was a dark-colored rotary phone. Oddly, it fit in with the rest of the atmosphere.

"Of course," Emma muttered under her breath. What else would be appropriate for such a creepy house? "Do we answer it?"

Spencer looked at her, seemingly amused. What was so funny, Emma didn't know.

He headed towards the phone, determination etched in his features. Too bad it didn't have a speakerphone.

"Hello?" He picked it up and placed it to his ear.

Emma inched closer, trying to eavesdrop without

getting noticed. This had something to do with Nick, or she'd eat her hat. It was just too much of a coincidence otherwise.

Spencer frowned, and his gaze flickered towards Emma. "No, you can talk to me." He seemed frustrated with whoever was on the other end of the line. "We don't negotiate."

Then Spencer swallowed thickly. He heard something on the other end of the line that frightened him. Was Nick getting hurt? Emma's heart raced.

"Let me talk to him." Emma caught herself off guard, but she meant what she said. She would do anything to save Nick. To save the world they had started building with each other.

Spencer seemed torn. Then he held the large end of the phone between the two of them. "Speak up," he told whoever was on the other end. "She's here."

"Hello?" Emma's voice felt quiet. She cleared her throat, straightened up. "This is Emma."

"Hello, Emma." The voice was silky-smooth and recognizable. It was Eric.

"What do you want?" Emma asked, with courage she wasn't sure she had.

"Oh, we'll get to that." He sounded nonchalant, as if it was just another casual phone call. "What's your favorite color, Emma?"

Emma stared at the phone as if it had sprouted horns.

Then she heard a smack, heard Nick's cry. Her stomach dropped.

"Answer the question," Eric said pleasantly.

"Light pink," Emma said, despite Spencer shaking his head. She didn't want Nick to get hurt, especially not because of her. "Why did you take her?"

At least they had confirmed who Nick had been taken by, and that she had been taken. Not that it made the situation any better.

"That's not important." He made a disapproving noise with his tongue. "Where did you go when you left? You were a local. You grew up in a nice home, just like me. An older home." His voice was dreamy now. "With your mother, and David, and -"

"David?" Emma said without intending to.

"Of course." He sounded surprised. "Your father."

The world fell out from underneath Emma. "How did you know that?" She whispered, gripping the phone even tighter.

Spencer looked at her, alarmed.

"I bet you looked nice with the blood in your hair," Eric said, his voice wistful. "Too bad I couldn't see it."

Emma felt like the world was freezing. Well, that answered the question of who'd attacked her. "Why?"

"You were trouble." It sounded like a shrug. "But, we've talked too long. You know where to find me." Then the line went dead.

Emma was staring into nothing, her eyes wide. Was

it the truth? Did he mean what he said? Surely he was lying. But how would he know that if he wasn't telling the truth? "He knew my father." Her words were almost a whisper.

Spencer's eyebrows went towards the ceiling, but Emma didn't care.

Sitting on the swing set, watching her mother, with two black eyes and numerous bruises, begging him to stay. "Please, David. Please, I'll do anything."

It broke Emma's heart to see her mother cry. To see her continue to love the one that hurt them. But she had tried to fix it before and nothing had helped.

She lowered her head, looking at the floor. Nothing would ever help.

"I think I know where he is."

THE DRIVE to Belle's House took at least five times longer than it usually did, Emma could have sworn. She was biting her nails now, twirling her fingers in her hair. Exhibiting any and every nervous habit that she had ever shown in her life.

"How do you know he's there?" Spencer was the one driving, with Emma in the passenger seat and Allison and other cars not too far behind.

It was a road Emma really didn't want to have to go down, but she would, for Nick. "My mother loved the man who abused her," she said. "He left when I was seven. He never came back."

"And?" Spencer waited.

"His name was David." Emma looked at her hands in her lap. "We never saw him again. I don't even know if he's alive or dead."

"Do you think this relates to the murders?" Spencer asked.

Emma shrugged helplessly. "Maybe. It may be why he was murdering people close to me. Or it may be a huge coincidence and it wasn't me he was targeting. I don't know."

Spencer tapped a finger against the steering wheel as he thought. "Okay. I want you to stay back when we get there, okay?" His voice was stern. "Your safety is our top priority."

"But -"

"No buts." His voice softened. "You need to stay alive and safe for Nick. When we get her out, she's going to need you."

Emma's hands clenched and then unclenched. "You say that like you're certain."

Spencer let out a long breath. "No matter what, we'll get her back."

Emma looked out the window. "I hope so."

CHAPTER TWENTY-NINE

Wednesday, September 21st, 2016. 9:03pm.

It was more than irritating to have blood dripping from a cut on her face and not be able to do anything about it with her bound hands. At least he had loosened them a little bit, so that her hands no longer felt like they were going to fall off. The blindfold had also come off, like he wanted her to see what happened next.

She had been forced to listen to the phone call, to him luring Emma. Why Belle's House? Why Emma? There were so many questions that Nick didn't know the answers to.

"I know, I know." There was a pleased quality to Eric's voice. "She's definitely coming." Eric came into view. He wasn't holding a phone, and his eyes weren't too far away.

Then he frowned, the scowl darkening his face. Nick was getting a glimpse of how he had treated Julia. "You'll never have her." Whoever he was talking to, or whoever he *thought* he was talking to, he didn't like them at the moment.

At that point, there was a decent chance he was crazy and talking to someone that didn't exist. Which wasn't good news for Nick. If he was crazy enough to be having a psychotic break, he was definitely crazy enough to kill.

As if, you know, the three murders didn't prove that already.

She started playing with her wrist restraints, tugging them this way and that while she tried to keep the rest of her body still. He had taken all of her weapons off her, but that wasn't going to stop her from trying. She had to escape. She had to get out of there and get back to Emma.

"Why did you do it?" she asked.

He blinked, confused. His attention shifted towards her. "What?"

"Kill the other two." They had already established Julia.

He shrugged. "Throw off the track." Then his lips curved into an evil grin. "Revenge."

Nick kept her face expressionless. "What do you mean?"

Eric's face was hard. "Sometimes people know

things they're not supposed to." His voice was cold. "And sometimes those people have to be eliminated."

"Melanie?" Nick glanced at him, then glanced away. "She knew too much?"

He answered with a quick nod. "She found the letters that Julia hid. She hoarded them." His lips curled into a snarl.

"And Rachel was just in the wrong place at the wrong time?" Nick's voice was bleak. That poor girl.

"If I killed someone else, then they'd stop looking for me." Eric shrugged. "And Rachel had plenty of enemies." He chuckled, as if it was funny.

"Why did you go after Emma?" Nick had to know.

Eric scoffed. "She was in the way." Then he smiled. "Now she'll be mine."

"You tried to take her out because she knew too much?" Nick kept her voice nonjudgmental.

Eric nodded, but he was clearly distracted. Then something out of the corner of his eye caught his attention. His face lit up like a boy getting his Christmas presents.

Dread curled in Nick's stomach. What was it? Was the person he was talking to finally arriving, or was it something else? As if the answers to her questions hadn't made her sick enough.

"They're here," he said, his voice breathless with excitement.

"Stay in the car." Spencer sounded exasperated.

"No." Emma's words were firm. "I'm not going to hide in the corner."

He just looked at her.

She was being stupid, and she knew it, but she doubted Eric was going to talk to them. She needed to be there in case he would only talk to her.

Spencer let out an exasperated sigh and tossed her a bulletproof vest. "Put that on," he ordered, "and stay back."

She nodded, quickly sticking her arms through it. How to secure it was another question.

"Here." Allison helped her, adjusting the straps.

"Thanks." Emma settled it across her body. It felt bulky but necessary. She definitely didn't want to save Nick just to die in the crossfire.

Spencer headed towards the door, shooting Emma a glare when she tried to follow. Instead she stood back by the car, hands on her hips and ears straining to hear any noise.

Spencer rapped on the door. As he shifted, Emma could see the bulletproof vest underneath his jacket.

She swallowed. It was serious. Even Spencer was worried. Was she really doing the right thing?

Apparently he got an invitation, because he cautiously opened the door and moved forward. Emma inched closer, hating herself for what she was doing. She was risking herself, risking Nick's life for interfering without permission.

But she bet that Eric was going to ask for her.

A shot rang out, and Allison tackled Emma and dropped her to the ground.

"Stand back!" Spencer shouted, his voice carrying outside. "Don't shoot."

Emma's heart was racing like a hummingbird's, her body starting to tremble.

But then a truckload of adrenaline washed over her, leaving her feeling awfully calm and collected. She stood up, thanking Allison with a smile. Then she started towards the door.

There was nothing like facing your own death to cause a person to think clearly.

She knew who Eric reminded her of. She knew why he looked familiar.

He looked like her father.

"Eric?" Emma pitched her voice higher, ignoring the dirty looks the police officers were shooting her. She was taking a stupid risk, and she knew it, but it was a wager she would make.

"Emma?" Eric sounded pleased. "Look, she came!"

Who was he talking to? She kept her face neutral, trying not to draw any more attention to herself than she already was. "Can I come in?"

"Are you armed?" he asked.

Emma glanced at herself. "No. I have a vest on."

"Come in."

She took a deep breath, shoving back the nerves, fear, the worry, and walked forward. She was either going to save Nick, or die trying.

It wasn't the most brilliant plan she had ever come up with in her life. Probably not the most stupid, but it ranked highly up there.

Eric came into view before anyone else. He had two guns in his hand. Spencer was standing to his left, arms up above his head and a red stain spreading from his shoulder.

"You're hurt," Emma said without thinking.

"Just a flesh wound," Spencer said without looking at her. She turned slightly, ignoring Eric to seek Nick.

When she met Nick's eyes, her knees almost collapsed in relief. Nick was okay. She wasn't perfect, but she was as okay as she had been when they were on the phone. No bullet holes, no nothing.

"Do you know who I am?" Eric's voice was soft.

Emma lifted her head to meet his steely gaze. She could see it now. The slope of his nose. The coldness of his eyes. "You're my brother."

Eric looked pleased. "Half-brother," he clarified. "Did you ever wonder why your daddy left?" He was mocking now.

Emma wasn't sure what to say, so she said nothing. It seemed safer in that moment.

"He had a whole different family." Eric seemed amused by this, as if he thought he was tormenting her. Did he think she actually liked her father? "Me, my brother, and our Mom."

Emma lifted her head, trying not to waver. "I didn't know that."

"He didn't tell us about you, of course." Eric seemed disappointed. "But I knew when I saw you. You look like him."

Well that was quickly filed under one of the worst things Emma had heard. "Thanks. You too."

He studied her, although he kept an eye on both Nick and Spencer. "You're coming with me," he said. "Even though you're here for her." He jerked his head in Nick's direction.

Emma looked at Nick, then back to Eric. "Why?"

"I'm going to have you for my own, of course." He looked at her, irritated that she hadn't followed his train of thought.

Guilt tugged at Emma, but she locked it away. Nick had been kidnapped because he was after *her*? She had put Nick in danger. She took a deep breath, trying to keep her mind in the here and now.

"Please let her go." Emma's voice was softer than she would have liked, but it didn't matter. "You can take me, but let her go."

Eric studied her, his eyes cold. Searching, as if trying to discover whether or not she was lying. And

Emma wasn't. She would have gladly traded herself for Nick.

She couldn't help but look at Nick, see the haggard exhaustion in her eyes, the way the ropes bit into her wrists. She would do anything to have her out of the house, safe and sound. Then her eyes drifted back to the man who had killed her ladies. The one who had endangered everything she had worked so hard for.

"Why did you kill them?" Emma kept her voice strong. Sure, the police could figure it out, but Emma wanted to hear it. She wanted to hear him say it.

"They were in the way." Eric chuckled.

"How?" Emma looked at him. "They didn't do anything to you."

Eric sighed. "I have an important job, you know." He looked at Spencer, then back at Emma. "I'm an important person. They're expendable."

It was only the gun in Eric's hand that kept Emma from rushing at him and trying to beat him with anything she could get her hands on.

"They deserved to live as much as you don't," Emma said through gritted teeth.

Eric laughed.

Emma saw red. "You bastard," she hissed.

A scowl passed over Eric's face, and the gun twitched in her direction.

Fear surged through Emma, but it kept her strong.

She wasn't going to let him get to her. If she died, so be it.

"Don't." Nick's voice was muffled, but Emma heard it.

"Shut up." Eric hit Nick with the butt of the gun. Her eyes rolled back into her head, and she collapsed.

Emma screamed, and a gun went off.

CHAPTER THIRTY

Wednesday, September 21st, 2016. 9:54pm.

The first thing Nick looked for when her eyes opened was Emma. Which wasn't hard, since Emma's face kind of crowded her vision. "Hi," Nick said, her voice weaker than she expected.

Well. Not that it was entirely unexpected after the whole kidnapping-and-beating thing.

Speaking of, where was the evil bastard?

"Is he dead?" Nick croaked.

"Yes." That was Spencer's voice. More people appeared, fussing over her and starting to put her on a stretcher.

"I'm fine." Nick scowled with as much energy as she could muster.

Emma just looked at her. Spencer's face was much the same.

Nick looked away. She would bluff better when she was feeling better. Significantly better.

At least she hadn't been shot. The only one who had fired was Spencer, who had taken Eric out before he could hurt Emma.

Or so Nick assumed from the chaos around them.

"You're going to the hospital," Spencer informed her.

"I'm fine." Nick tried to sit up.

Ouch, that was a bad decision. She quickly laid back on the stretcher.

"Exactly." Emma and Spencer exchanged looks.

Great. Now Nick had two babysitters.

Allison came towards them, close enough so that Nick could see her. "They finished searching Eric's house," she said, her voice directed towards Spencer.

"And?" Spencer looked extra curious.

Nick struggled to pay attention around the fog clouding her mind. "What?"

"We found a dead body in a basement freezer." Allison seemed either mildly disturbed or amused, Nick wasn't entirely certain.

"What?" Nick struggled to sit up again, aborting the action after her head spun. That was less than pleasant.

"It was a male. Based on identification found with the body, we think it's Eric's brother." Allison kept her voice professional. "He's been dead at least a week."

Nick would have rocked back on her heels if that had been possible. Instead, she just leaned back into the stretcher.

"Eric's wife and son were found locked in a sound-proof room off the basement. Both were filthy and starving, and are willing to testify to Eric putting them in there." Allison swallowed thickly, clearly not pleased with the whole 9-year-old stuck in a dark box thing.

"We also found this on Eric's body." She extended her hand towards Spencer.

Spencer looked at it, then passed the cell phone to Emma.

Emma took it, looking uncertainly at them. Then she opened the phone, checked the contacts, and her eyes widened. "It's Julia's."

Spencer turned to look at Nick. "You were right that she had another phone. But he took it with him."

Nick didn't know what to say. She wasn't entirely certain if she could speak. Emma had slipped her hand into Nick's and was holding it tight.

The situation became too much. Nick, stalwart in the face of whatever came, tried to stop the tears leaking down her face. Not that, objectively, she could blame herself, with the whole kidnapping and her girl-friend almost dying and everything, but it was embarrassing.

"Get her to the hospital." Spencer slapped Nick's

shoulder gently, affectionately, and then gestured to the medical personnel. "Emma will be going with her."

Emma looked at him, then apparently decided not to argue, because she got into the ambulance, her hand still clutching Nick's.

"I'm fine," Nick insisted, although who she was talking to she wasn't entirely certain. Or if she was talking to someone, she doubted they were listening.

"You're going to be evaluated for a concussion," one of the EMTs said cheerfully.

Nick scowled at the ceiling of the ambulance. Exactly how she wanted to spend her evening.

"Please." Emma's voice was soft, and Nick melted.

It was easy to settle after that, to let her eyes drift close. Her eyelids were awfully heavy, after all, and she was helping Emma by getting some rest and making sure she was fine.

"We're here." The EMT's voice drew Nick back to consciousness, and she struggled to clear the fog following her nap.

Nick felt strangely alone when Emma let go of her hand for the EMTs to get the gurney out of the ambulance and roll it into the ER. It was like she was missing something, like there was a ghost hand that should have been there.

It felt strangely childlike to miss someone. She hadn't felt that way since Sarah had died, since she had slept for months on her side of the bed, missing that comforting presence on the other side.

"In here." Nick was mostly dignified as she was moved from the ambulance stretcher to the hospital's, even though it hurt.

Then Emma took her hand back and everything was okay again for the moment.

"We'll have to take you to get an MRI, but we'll do the stitches first." The EMTs seemed amused. Nick ignored them.

She turned her attention to Emma. "Are you okay?" Nick asked, needing to know the answer to the question.

Emma raised her eyebrows. "I should be asking you that question," she said pointedly. "Miss I-got-kidnapped-and-then-hit-over-the-head."

"I'm fine!" Nick looked down at herself, the movement exaggerated. "I'm even in one piece."

Emma rolled her eyes, but there was a hint of a smile on her face. Then it faded, exhaustion replacing it. "I thought…"

"I know." Nick swallowed thickly, not able to voice the words that lurked deep in her mind.

I almost lost you.

I thought I had lost you.

She knew what it was like to be that alone, and she never wanted to feel that way again. She never wanted Emma to feel that way.

"I love you." Nick was the first one to say it, but it was something she had felt for a long time.

Emma leaned down and pressed a kiss to Nick's lips as carefully as she could. "I love you too," she said softly. "But if you ever do this again, I'll kill you."

Even Nick could appreciate that. She laughed, too.

"They called me to do the stitches." Jordan's voice caught Nick off guard. Not that Nick could spin around and look for her, anyway.

"Yes, because they require the ICU doctor to do simple stitches." Nick raised her eyebrows. "That makes sense."

"The ER doctors won't work with you because you're ornery," Jordan said simply.

Nick wasn't sure if it was a joke. After all, she'd only gone to the ER a few times before. Surely she wasn't that bad.

Jordan pulled a stitching kit out, and Nick glared at it. Was she bleeding, still? She hadn't noticed.

"Your head." Emma smoothed some hair back, as careful as she could. "When he hit you with the gun, it cut you. Worse than your prior cut."

"Great," Nick muttered.

Emma smiled, and Nick felt that warm fluttering that swam through her whenever Emma looked at her like that. It was a feeling she had missed.

"I'll make sure she takes care of herself," Emma promised.

Nick looked offended.

"And make sure she picks her dog up, she's driving the horse crazy." Jordan grinned.

Nick rolled her eyes. Her life was crazy, yes, but she wouldn't change it for the world.

EPILOGUE

Nick pulled her cruiser up to Belle's House. She could see the construction crews working, Emma standing outside barking orders. When she decided to do something, she did it full force.

That was something Nick loved about her.

Emma turned and caught sight of her car. The smile she gave Nick made her stomach flip.

Emma said something else to the workers, then dropped whatever she was doing and headed in Nick's direction.

"Hello," Emma said, her eyes soft.

"Having fun?" Nick drawled.

"Tons." Emma glanced back towards the construction. "What's up?"

Nick reached into her cruiser, pulling out a small cooler. "Got time for lunch?"

Then Lady Grey raced out from behind the builders, heading straight for Nick.

From years of practice, Nick settled her stance, making sure that she couldn't knock her over. Instead, Lady Grey barked and howled and jumped, demonstrating her approval at Nick's existence.

"She missed you," Emma said wryly.

"Apparently." Nick grinned at her. "Is there a place to sit?"

"There's shade under the tree." Emma grabbed the cooler, heading towards the aforementioned tree. Nick followed, her gaze taking in everything around her. Belle's House even felt brighter, sun shining on it as if it knew it was a new day and a new world.

It would no longer be a safe haven, but it would provide a different function. They would keep the security, rebuild the damage that had been done by Eric, and turn it into a halfway home for domestic violence victims.

"Here." Emma sat the cooler down, sinking into a cross-legged position on the grass. Nick settled next to her, ignoring the grass that would get on her slacks.

"Can we join?" Carys's voice startled Nick, but she nodded.

"They asked if they could help." Emma's eyes glinted.

Nick rolled her eyes, but she was smiling. Jordan

and Carys came over, settling onto the grass with them. They had their own lunch boxes.

"Sandwiches for everyone, it seems," Jordan observed.

"They're good!" Emma said defensively.

Carys laughed.

Nick couldn't help raising a smile. Her life had changed so much in a few short weeks. She had Emma - her girlfriend, and maybe, in the future, her wife. She had friends, she had a job she loved and people that cared about her.

"So have you guys decided what you're doing?" Jordan asked innocently, taking a bite of her sandwich.

Nick looked at her, then Emma. "What?"

"With where you're going to live." Jordan said innocently. "With the whole 'your house burned down' and stuff."

"We're going to get a place of our own," Emma said before Nick could say anything.

"What?" Nick blinked at her, somewhat blindsided. Not that she didn't agree with that idea, or didn't want it, but she hadn't exactly expected it to be decided like that.

"If that's okay with you." Emma turned to look at her. Her eyes were shining, her curly hair moving with the wind. There was an affection there, a love, that made Nick's heart ache with love for her.

"Of course," Nick said. And it was. There were far

worse things than moving in with Emma, wherever they ended up.

"And maybe we can turn it into a shelter." Emma trailed off thoughtfully.

Nick held up a finger. "Woah there," she said, laughing. "One step at a time!"

Emma grinned, bumping her shoulder against Nick's, and the group broke out into laughter.

Nick's heart swelled. "I love you," she murmured to Emma.

"I love you too." Emma kissed her. "Now finish your sandwich."

HI READER!

"Necessary Sacrifice" is my fourth book, and I hope you enjoyed reading it as much as I did writing it! Keep reading, there's a couple PREVIEW CHAPTERS of my newest book, "Remember Me", after this!! Whether you're a repeat reader or someone new to my work, I am really grateful that you took time out of your busy day to read my book! It would mean a lot to me if you could take a minute and leave a review of Necessary Sacrifice on Amazon, or even Goodreads. Reviews make a big difference in the success of a new book/author, and I really want to know what my readers think and what they would like to see more of! If you like this book and haven't yet read my other books, you can find them here:

<u>Shattered Hearts</u>

Falling For You,

I Spy (featuring Jordan and Carys)!

Poker Face

Remember Me

If you want to see sneak peeks into my books and into my life, please follow me at facebook.com/noellewintersbooks. Each new book will be released at 3.99 for the first 24 hours and I send out a special notification to my mailing list/FB page! If you would like to be notified when a book is freshly released, please please please sign up for my newsletter here:

http://eepurl.com/cwCSub

or like my Facebook page here:

https://www.facebook.com/noellewintersbooks/

Also - feel free to drop me an email at noellewintersbooks@gmail.com! Or a message on my FB page! I love hearing from you. It makes a writer's day, that's for sure. :)

I hope you are well, dear reader, and I hope to see you again soon!

Noelle

REMEMBER ME

CHAPTER ONE

January 21st, 2014. 10:34am.

Katy sat on the bench, her back aching from carrying Tally all the way to the park. She sat the cooler down next to her feet, her purse next to it, and watched Tally as she ran up to the play structure. It was chilly for Arizona, so Katy had dressed her in a loud red jacket. Something easy to see from far away. She wouldn't need it in a few hours when the chill was gone, but for now it kept her warm.

Tally was four, and time had passed so fast. Tally looked just like her, too. The same brown hair, same light ringlets. Same blue eyes. The slightly too-big nose, but a warm expression that brightened even the darkest of corners. Katy found her heart swelling every time she looked at her daughter, overwhelmed by the protective instincts that swamped her.

No one had prepared her for motherhood, not even her own mother. Then again, her Mom and Dad had abandoned her when she had decided she was going to keep her daughter. So much for Catholics sticking with family. She took a deep breath and consciously unclenched her hands; her nails had been digging into the meat of her palms. It had been four years. She had bigger priorities now.

Katy leaned back against the wood of the bench, watching Tally as she headed up the stairs to the top of the slide. It was chilly for January, something that always amused her. She had lived in Oregon until she was nine, and in January, people would be in shorts with highs in the 60s. Here all the natives were bundled up.

The playground was covered by a large awning, something standard for Arizona where the summers could easily hit 115 degrees. There was nothing fun about burning yourself when attempting to play. Swings were off to the side, slides spiraling out of the structure itself at random intervals. For a while, Katy lost herself in watching her daughter. The joy, the laughter - everything that made Katy's heart swell with pride.

She glanced at her watch. It was just after noon. Lunch time. She'd probably need the jacket off, too. Katy looked up, searching for the red jacket. Tally was standing at the top of the slide, her eyes wide and her brown hair sticking out from underneath the woolen cap.

She glanced down at her picnic bag, reaching down to pull out the sandwiches she had prepared. Meat and cheese for herself, peanut butter and light on the jelly for Tally. Plus carrots and dip. Anything and everything she could use to tempt her picky eater.

"Do you have a Band-Aid?" Another woman caught her attention. The mom was flushed, her hair tossed up in a messy bun, and she was dressed in yoga pants and a hoodie. There was a two-year-old on her hip, whose eyes were red from crying and who looked seconds from bursting into further tears. Katy more than sympathized. It was only in the last year or so that she'd managed to leave the house in something other than sweats.

She bent down, digging through her purse. "Is Hello Kitty okay?"

The mom laughed in relief, taking it and showing the little girl in her arms. "It's her favorite. Thank you."

Katy smiled at her. "No problem." She glanced up, searching for the red jacket and finding Tally near the monkey bars this time. Part of Katy wanted to rush over there and catch her, make sure she wasn't doing anything dangerous. But Tally was old enough that she'd complain, hands on her hips as she shot Katy *the glare* about how she was a big girl now. She was getting big. Katy didn't want to think about it. Soon she'd be starting kindergarten.

She pulled out the last of their lunch, placing it on a cloth napkin on the bench she had been sitting on. The sky was bright and blue, sun beaming down on them and warming the cold weather. A glance up at her told her that Tally had lost the wool hat. Katy sighed. It was the third one that month.

"Tally!" Katy called, standing and turning towards the play structure. She wasn't that far away, maybe fifteen feet, but it was far enough that Tally was going to practice her selective listening skills. Katy sighed in exasperation, her hands on her hips. "Tally, come here!"

The red jacket kept going, heading up towards the slide again. Glancing back at her purse and their lunch, Katy headed towards the playground, watching Tally as she slid down the spiral slide, the exit pointing away from where Katy was.

"C'mere, you goofball." Katy's words were affectionate as she rounded the corner, heading to the exit of the slide. She grabbed Tally's hand, only to stare in surprise as Tally yanked it out of her grasp.

Then it hit her. The eyes looking back at her weren't Tally's. It was the same jacket, the same color hair. But it wasn't her daughter.

Maybe it was a coincidence. Katy stood straighter, stepping back a few feet and scanning the rest of the playground. No sign of another red jacket. Or of the pink shirt Tally had worn that morning, or the woolen hat.

"Did someone give you that jacket?" Katy turned to the little girl, aware that her voice was probably a bit too frantic. The child squirmed out of her grasp and ran away, leaving Katy standing there, in shock, by the slide. People were probably staring at her, but she didn't care.

"Tally!" Katy headed away from the playground, her eyes searching the nearby area. There was no fence, not a ton of foliage, so there wasn't anywhere she could have hidden without being seen, at least outside of the play structure. Right? She had to be somewhere, playing a game of hide and seek.

"Are you okay?" A mom pushing a stroller came up to her, concern in her evergreen eyes.

"I can't find my daughter." The words caught in Katy's throat. "Her name is Tally. She's four, brown hair and blue eyes. She was wearing a red jacket and a pink shirt under it."

"I'll help you look." The mom nodded, then pushed her stroller off in the opposite direction of Katy. Katy could hear her calling out to others, probably mobilizing the parents of the playground. Katy could barely hear the words, much less understand them.

It was like the world was spinning in circles, like a camera in a movie that was circling its point of view.

There was no glimpse of red. There was nothing. "Tally!"

"I called 911." It was the mom she had given the Hello Kitty Band-Aid to earlier, her two-year-old still fixed against her hip.

"Thanks," Katy said, trying not to sound ungrateful. Not that she was, but it didn't seem real. She didn't need 911, because her daughter wasn't missing. Surely Tally had just wandered off somewhere, and she would soon pop out and cry 'surprise!', waiting to see the happiness on her mom's face.

But there was no surprise. Instead the police came, and Katy was relegated to answering questions instead of searching for her child. Even as the police talked to her, and she talked back, all she could focus on was the mantra in her head, the voice that was silently chanting *she's gone, she's gone, she's gone.*

They had to find her.

They *had* to.

CHAPTER TWO

July 17ᵗʰ, 2014. 2:12pm.

Katy sat in the armchair, her face blank. Sitting across from her was Special Agent Kiernan Mitchell, his eyes serious. It had been six months, six months of hell. Tally had never been found. Countless leads had been pursued. And all Katy could think was that it was her fault.

If only she had been watching Tally better. If only she hadn't brought lunch. *If only, if only.*

The FBI agent cleared his throat, drawing Katy's attention. "As I was saying, the next step is to continue working with local law enforcement, and pursuing leads as they come up."

Katy nodded numbly. She didn't know what to say. Was there even anything to say? She looked over at the red jacket hanging on the wall, a duplicate of the one Tally had been wearing that day. The real one was kept in evidence, just in case it was needed.

"Katy?" Kiernan's voice was gentle, something Katy appreciated. He and his team had been there for the first couple of months, and he had stayed longer to supervise. Surely they had been needed elsewhere.

"What are our next steps?" Katy dragged her attention back to him. He was older, probably late 50s, with salt-and-pepper hair and a warm, rugged face. He didn't seem used to Arizona's weather, much less Arizona in the summer.

Kiernan passed her a business card. "Do you remember Detective Rydell?"

"Greg?" Most of the detectives had given her their first names after the first two months had passed. It made it easier to reach out to them, easier to talk to them.

"Yes." Kiernan's eyes pierced hers. "If you need anything, if you remember anything or hear anything, give him a call. I'm sure you already have the number, but keep it just in case." Kiernan paused, then extended another business card to her. "You can always call me, if you need to. This is my personal office line."

Katy looked at him, met his eyes, and nodded a tired nod. She still clung to hope that she would find Tally eventually, that somehow, someday, she would come home. She was smart enough to know that the odds weren't good. That the likelihood of Tally coming home alive shrank every day. Sure, something told her that Tally was still alive. But was there actually something to it, or was it wishful thinking?

She shoved the thoughts out of her mind. Those were for when she was lying in bed, staring at the wall, and not able to fight them off. Depression was a bitch, and hers had come back with a vengeance.

"Thank you for everything you've done," Katy said, and she meant it.

Kiernan nodded to her, then stood. "Take care, Katy."

Katy smiled tiredly at him. Or as much of a smile as she could manage. She hadn't been able to work in months. Some days she barely left her bed. How did others do it, losing a child? How did they not stay comatose for the rest of their lives?

She didn't notice when he left. Instead she was staring at Greg's business card. He had been part of the investigation since Tally had disappeared, and she liked him. He was now in charge of finding her missing daughter, the one whose kidnapper had eluded police for so long.

Instead of dialing Greg, she dialed her friends instead. Maybe Lucia and Eleanor would be able to come over for dinner and a movie. Something to distract her from the fact there was nothing more she could do.

**

Check out "Remember Me" to read the rest!

Made in the USA
Columbia, SC
19 December 2018